# The Golden
## Concise Encyclopedia of
# MAMMALS

AN ILEX BOOK

Copyright © 1992 Ilex Publishers Limited

Illustrated by Jim Channell, John Francis, George Fryer
Robert Morton, Colin Newman – Bernard Thornton Artists,
Julie Carpenter, Ron Hayward Art Group,
Hussain Hussain, Aziz Khan.

Designed by Ted Kinsey

Created and produced by Ilex Publishers Limited,
29-31 George Street, Oxford OX1 2AJ

Color separation by Eray Scan Pte. Ltd.
Printed in Spain by Cronion S.A.

# The Golden
# Concise Encyclopedia of
# MAMMALS

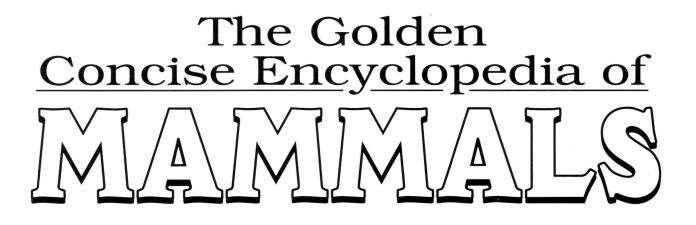

## By David Lambert

A GOLDEN BOOK ● NEW YORK
Western Publishing Company, Inc., Racine, Wisconsin 53404

# Contents

# Introduction

Mammals are among the most varied of all animals. Of the millions of kinds of animals alive today, about 4,000 are mammals. Shrews, and bats the size of bees, are the smallest mammals. The biggest animal of all time is the blue whale. There are mammals that live for two years or less, and others that can live for up to 70 years or more. Mammals can be found everywhere, from the snowy Arctic to hot deserts, oceans, swamps, forests, and even cities.

## CHARACTERISTICS OF MAMMALS

Mammals get their name from the special glands the females have called "mammae." These glands produce the milk that their young feed on. Mammals are vertebrates. This means that they have backbones. They are warm-blooded, and all have at least some hair.

Mammals have certain advantages over other animals. They produce body heat quickly by "burning up" the food stored inside their bodies. Their hairy coats help prevent this warmth from being lost. Because they can keep warm in this way, mammals can stay active in weather that is cold enough to make a snake or any other cold-blooded animal too sluggish to move. Most unborn mammals develop safely inside their mothers' bodies, and all are fed and cared for right after birth. A single baby chimpanzee has a better chance of living to be an adult than a thousand baby fish hatched out unprotected in the open sea. Lastly, most mammals have more developed brains than do other creatures. Instead of behaving only by instinct, they can *learn* how to cope with the world around them. Among the most intelligent of all animals are dogs, seals, whales, monkeys, apes — and humans!

## HOW MAMMALS EVOLVED

Mammals were not always as numerous and varied as they are now. About 200 million years ago the first mammals were shy, mouselike creatures. Their ancestors were small reptiles. The early mammals had to hide from the dinosaurs. No mammal too big to burrow or to climb trees could have survived alongside the many fierce, giant species of dinosaurs. But the dinosaurs died out about 65 million years ago. At that time, mammals were evolving, or changing. By 40 million years ago all the main groups of living mammals had appeared, along with some that would become extinct.

## THE FAMILY TREE OF MAMMALS

Scientists divide living mammals into three groups: the egg-layers, or monotremes; the pouched mammals, or marsupials; and the placental mammals. Most mammals today are

placental mammals, nourished by a placenta inside their mother's body until birth. This book looks at each main group in turn. The family tree of mammals at the end of this introduction shows how the groups are formed. The main branches of the mammal family tree are the groups called "orders." These include large groups such as insectivores (insect-eaters), bats, primates, and carnivores (meat-eaters). Each of these orders contains mammal families. For instance, the order of carnivores includes the dog family and the raccoon family. Each mammal family is made up of genera. Each genus (sing.) contains different kinds, or species. For instance, the raccoon genus *Procyon* includes the species *Procyon lotor* (the North American raccoon) and *Procyon cancrivorus* (the crab-eating raccoon). Species like these form the "twigs" on the complete family tree of mammals.

**HOW MAMMALS HAVE ADAPTED**
Although all mammals are similar in many ways, each species has evolved a unique lifestyle to help it survive in its own habitat. The polar bear's thick fur protects it from the intense Arctic cold. The harp seal stays warm thanks to thick body fat. A dromedary's long legs and a fennec fox's long ears throw off excess body heat, which is how these mammals can survive in hot deserts.

Animals must be able to move, in order to find food or to escape from enemies. Mammals depend on their limbs for survival. Moles burrow with their powerful front paws. Long-legged kangaroos and horses leap or gallop over open grassland. Monkeys climb, with help from grasping toes and fingers. Bats fly on wings of skin stretched between the bones of their fingers, arms, and legs. In the water, seals and whales steer and brake with flippers.

Each mammal has a digestive system that is suited to the food it eats. Lions, dogs, and other meat-eaters have sharp teeth that slice through flesh. Plant-eaters such as cows and horses have broad, flat teeth for grinding leaves to a pulp, and a long, complex gut to digest the pulp.

Many mammals have body parts that serve as built-in weapons to attack rivals or their prey. Cats have sharp teeth and claws, and male stags fight each other with their antlers. Some mammals that are eaten by other animals have evolved body parts that serve as defense mechanisms. For example, porcupines have sharp spines called quills. But many mammals avoid their enemies by running fast or by hiding in trees or in burrows.

Mammals have different ways of communicating with others of their kind. Wolves howl, and certain

antelopes mark tree branches with scent from glands below their eyes. Such signals help male and female mammals meet and mate.

**WHERE MAMMALS LIVE**
Signals also help mammals mark out the edges of their territory. Many male mammals claim a piece of ground and drive out rival males that stray inside it. Others stay on the move to find food or to escape the cold of winter. In fall, mountain sheep move down to the warm valleys, and gray whales swim several thousand miles south to warmer waters.

Scientists divide the world into different regions, each with its own special groups of animals. Long ago, spreading seas or rising mountain chains cut off certain mammals from their relatives on other continents, and the separated groups evolved in different ways. Now all monotremes and most marsupials live only in or around Australia. Certain monkeys and sloths live only in South and Central America. Most antelopes live in Africa, and the lemurs live nowhere outside the island of Madagascar. Pronghorns are found only in North America.

**MAMMALS AT RISK**
Some mammal groups have multiplied, but many others have grown scarce.

There are hundreds of species of bats and rodents, for example, but only five species of rhinoceros and one species of wild horse. Altogether, nearly 700 species and subspecies, or varieties, of mammal, are rare enough for scientists to think that they could die out altogether. (This book will indicate if a species is seriously threatened.)

Almost all the mammals in danger are now threatened by just one species: our own. Mammals in the wild disappear as people destroy habitats by chopping down forests, draining swamps, or building roads and cities in the countryside. Some rare species are trapped or hunted; others are poisoned by agricultural chemicals that are washed into rivers, lakes, and seas.

Conservationists have saved some rare mammals, such as the Arabian oryx and the golden lion tamarin, by capturing them and breeding them in zoos. The best way to save mammals, though, is by protecting their habitats. Governments may set aside forests, grasslands, and marshes as nature reserves.

Earth would be a far duller planet without these threatened species. They are important links in the rich and varied world of mammals.

# The family tree of mammals

**Millions of years**

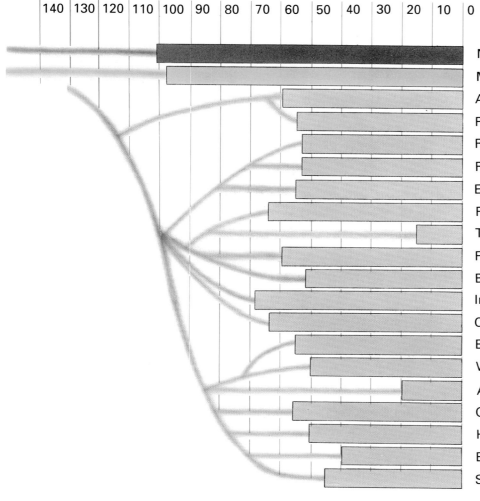

| 140 | 130 | 120 | 110 | 100 | 90 | 80 | 70 | 60 | 50 | 40 | 30 | 20 | 10 | 0 |

Monotremes

Marsupials

Anteaters, sloths, and armadillos

Pangolins

Rabbits, hares, and pikas

Rodents

Elephant shrews

Primates

Tree shrews

Flying lemurs

Bats

Insectivores

Carnivores

Even-toed hoofed mammals

Whales

Aardvarks

Odd-toed hoofed mammals

Hyraxes

Elephants

Sea cows

The branches on this family tree show approximately when each main group of living mammals appeared on earth and how different groups are related. Scientists first worked out these relationships by comparing the teeth and bones of living mammals with those of their long-dead ancestors. Two kinds of mammals with very similar teeth are likely to be close relatives. Now experts can also match DNA—the tiny molecules within the cells that determine a creature's species; skin, eye, and hair color; sex; and so on. This, plus new fossil finds, sometimes produce surprises. Not all similar-looking groups of mammals are close relatives. Cows and horses are both hoofed land mammals, yet cows are more like whales than horses! Also, some mammals have been put in the wrong order or family. For example, several scientists now suspect that guinea pigs are not rodents at all. Experts will continue to update the family tree as more information becomes available.

On this family tree, the thin lines show how scientists *believe* the groups fit together. The dates shown by the wider lines are based on evidence from fossil finds.

# Monotremes and marsupials

Monotremes are mammals that lay eggs, like birds and reptiles, but feed their young milk, like other mammals. The only monotremes still alive today are the platypus and two kinds of echidnas, or spiny anteaters.

Marsupials are mammals that give birth to tiny babies that continue to develop in a pouch on their mother's belly. There are about 250 kinds of marsupials. Only one marsupial, the common or Virginia opossum, lives in the United States. About 70 species of opossums live in Mexico and Central and South America. All other marsupials, including kangaroos, phalangers, and possums, live in or near Australia. Monotremes and marsupials are primitive mammals. They have survived mostly because the sea isolated them from more modern animals that might have killed them off.

**Greater glider**   About 3 feet long, this phalanger glides from tree to tree. As it jumps out into the air, with its arms and legs spread, a flap of skin is stretched out between its front (fore) and back (hind) limbs. This "parachute" helps the mammal to glide as much as 350 feet from one tree to another. With each jump it loses height, and so it must scamper up the tree it lands on before making the next jump. Greater gliders live in the forests of eastern Australia. They feed at night on eucalyptus leaves.

**Spotted cuscus**   Early travelers to New Guinea and northeastern Australia mistook this large-eyed, slow-moving marsupial for a monkey. Usually its long tail is coiled up like a spring, but both its tail and hind feet can grip a branch while the cuscus hangs upside down to feed on leaves. The male spotted cuscus has an exceptionally striking coat. Its dark blotches camouflage it in the dappled forest light. Females are solid brown, fawn, or gray and so were once thought to belong to another species.

**Koala**   With its rounded head and ears, large black nose, furry body, and tiny tail, a koala looks very friendly and cuddly. Yet, before the Australian government protected koalas, hunters killed thousands of them for their fur. Shooting koalas was easy because they spend most of their lives perched high in eucalyptus trees, asleep or munching on the leaves that make them smell like mentholated cough drops. Koalas climb down only to move from one tree to another. The female's pouch opens to the rear, rather than to the front.

**Brush-tailed possum**   While most marsupials are becoming scarce, the brush-tailed possums are multiplying. The secret of their success is their varied diet and their willingness to live near people. In the wild, brush-tailed possums usually live in trees and feed on flowers, fruits, and leaves. Now many of these fox-sized animals live in towns, sleeping on roofs by day and prowling the streets at night to find food scraps. Originally from Australia, they were introduced into New Zealand, where they became pests in orchards.

**Platypus**   When a museum keeper first saw the skin of a platypus, he thought someone had sewed a duck's beak onto a mammal's furry body. The platypus, or duckbill, even has webbed feet, like a duck's. The short, furred tail is broad and flat, like a beaver's. Although the females lay tiny eggs in riverbank burrows, they feed their newborns milk. These strange monotremes swim in the streams of Tasmania and southeastern Australia, where they grub for tiny creatures in the mud with their sensitive, toothless beaks. A poisonous spur on each hind foot may help the male to catch frogs.

**Mouse possum**   This tiny marsupial with big, bulging eyes is the smallest of all possums. Five or six mouse possums could easily fit on a person's hand. Several species live in both rainy and dry Australian forests. By day, they sleep inside trees or logs, curled up in crevices. At night, they hunt for food — catching insects, eating pollen, and drinking sap and nectar. A mouse possum, also called the pygmy possum, can store food as fat inside its swollen, almost hairless tail. In cold weather, mouse possums become so drowsy that they don't fuss even if you pick them up.

**Spiny anteater**   Another name for the spiny anteater is the echidna. It rips open ant and termite nests with its strong claws. It then opens its toothless snout and flicks out a long, sticky tongue to catch the insects. Sharp spines between the hairs on its coat protect this monotreme from most enemies. A threatened echidna may curl up in a ball with only its spines exposed. It can also burrow at high speed. Each female lays one egg and incubates it in her belly pouch.

**Yellow-footed rock wallaby**
Not much bigger than a rabbit, this creature is far smaller than the great kangaroos, its close relatives. Known also as the ring-tailed rock wallaby, it is rather pretty, with yellowish markings on its limbs and tail. The yellow-footed rock wallaby inhabits rugged terrain, such as fallen rocks at the bottom of cliffs, in eastern and southeastern Australia. Somehow, in this harsh land, rock wallabies find enough to eat. They prefer grass but also feed on roots and bark. Foxes sometimes catch them, but rock wallabies are very agile mountaineers. They have long legs and rough-skinned feet that can grip smooth rock at least as well as rubber-soled shoes can. A climbing wallaby uses only its hind limbs, balancing itself with its tail. It leaps from rock to rock at high speed, jumping gaps 12 feet wide. A rock wallaby can even bound up a tree or sheer cliff.

**Red kangaroo** This is the largest kangaroo, the largest marsupial, and the largest Australian mammal. A male red kangaroo can be 7 feet tall and weigh about 200 pounds. Females are smaller. The males are usually reddish in color, but the females and about one male in three are bluish gray. Red kangaroos roam Australia's dry plains in groups called "mobs." The mobs are led by males known as "old men." An old man will punch and kick young male kangaroos, known as "bucks," to show who is in charge. Sometimes these kangaroos must travel far and fast to find enough water or plants to live on. They don't run, but bound along easily on their big, strong legs, balanced by a long, thick tail. They usually travel at about 8 miles per hour but can reach more than 30 miles per hour in short bursts. Red kangaroos are great jumpers, too. They have been known to make leaps of more than 40 feet. They can also make vertical leaps of up to 10 feet.

**Tasmanian devil** Early European settlers gave this name to the ferocious marsupial they found on the island of Tasmania. The bearlike "devil," about the size of a bull terrier, has a large head, a thick neck, powerful, sharp-toothed jaws, and a fierce growl. Determined Tasmanian devils have earned a bad reputation for breaking into chicken coops and killing entire flocks of chickens. Sometimes hungry individuals attack wallabies, which are larger than themselves, but usually these savage animals kill smaller prey or feed on animals already dead.

**Hairy-nosed wombat**
Wombats look somewhat like small bears. Some people call them Australian badgers because they use their strong claws to dig the long, deep burrows where they sleep. Largest of the three living species is the hairy-nosed wombat, which may weigh up to 60 pounds. It has a stocky body, a large head with fine hair covering its nose, and long, beaverlike front teeth. The hairy-nosed wombat, a plant-eater, lives in southern Australia, where the countryside is dry and scrubby. Because it does not sweat, it loses very little body water. This helps it to survive.

**Numbat** The numbat, or banded anteater, is the marsupial equivalent of the placental anteaters found in other regions of the world. With its sharp claws, the numbat rips open termite colonies in soil or rotten wood, thrusts its long, pointed muzzle inside, and captures the insects with its long, sticky tongue. The true anteaters are toothless, but a numbat has 52 teeth — more than any other mammal except some whales. A numbat can gobble up an incredible number of termites in a single day— up to 20,000.
***Threatened Species***

**Red-legged pademelon**
This wallaby, which measures about 3 feet long, has a thick tail and broad front teeth notched at the rear. Its name may come from *paddymalla*, an aborigine word for small kangaroos that live in scrub. The red-legged pademelon has reddish-brown upper parts, a yellow stripe on its hip, and reddish hind limbs. It is pale underneath. Like other pademelons, it is active at night, moving through tunnels burrowed in the undergrowth. Red-legged pademelons live in the warm, rainy forests of Queensland, Australia, and southeastern New Guinea.

**Quokka** One of the smallest of all wallabies, the quokka might easily be mistaken for a large rat. Its small, tapering tail gives this marsupial its other name of short-tailed wallaby. There were once many quokkas on the mainland of southwestern Australia. Now they are numerous only on small offshore islands nearby. Nibbling tree seedlings and making paths through the vegetation, quokkas keep themselves cool in hot weather by licking their fur. They do not sweat, but evaporation from their mouths (panting) takes some of the heat away from their bodies.

**Brush-tailed or red-tailed phascogale** This oddly named mouselike marsupial also goes by the name of common wambenger. Whatever you call it, this small tree-climber has an immensely long tail ending in a brush that looks somewhat like a feather duster. Its body is blue-gray, while its tail is black. The brush-tailed phascogale eats many kinds of food, ranging from nectar to bugs, mice, rats, and even ducks or other birds. It is widely distributed throughout Australia, but its population has been greatly reduced, mainly due to competition with rabbits that were brought in.

# Insectivores

The animals on these and all the following pages of this book are placental mammals. An organ called a placenta nourishes the unborn baby inside its mother's body, so that the young are more developed at birth than are newborn marsupials or monotremes.

Insectivores are small, somewhat primitive placental mammals. They have sharp teeth for crunching up even smaller animals, such as insects and worms. More than 350 kinds of insectivores exist; they can be found on all continents except Antarctica and Australia. Scientists often divide insectivores into six families — moles, shrews, hedgehogs, golden moles, solenodons, and tenrecs.

**Water shrew**  Water shrews look like silvery bubbles as they zoom around beneath the surface of a lake or stream. This is because they have a layer of air trapped by their fur. These determined little hunters can dive down to the bottom of a lake or stream and walk around searching for insects, worms, snails, and other aquatic prey. Their red-tipped teeth deliver a bite poisonous enough to kill a small fish or frog. Each day a water shrew must eat its own weight in food to keep from starving.

**Least shrew**  One of the world's smallest mammals, the least shrew is only slighter larger than a large bee. It lives in the damp evergreen forests of northern Europe and Asia. Least shrews must eat continually to replace the energy their bodies use up in simply keeping warm. For every three hours spent resting, a shrew must spend the next three scurrying through tunnels in grass or fallen leaves hunting for worms or other small prey. Even with enough food, shrews die of old age within about 15 months.

**Solenodon**  Two kinds of solenodons are found in the Caribbean — one in Cuba and the other in Haiti. Both look a bit like rat-sized shrews, with a long and pointed snout, tiny ears and eyes, sharp-clawed toes, and an almost hairless tail. They eat anything from roots and fruits to worms and lizards. Solenodons can deliver a poisonous bite, but they are unable to run away fast enough to escape dogs, cats, or other enemies. As a result, these strange insectivores are now very rare.
***Threatened Species***

**Forest elephant shrew**  Said to look like a miniature kangaroo with a tiny elephant's trunk, forest elephant shrews live in East and Central Africa. They might be more closely related to rabbits than to true insectivores. The largest species resembles a hunch-backed, long-legged rat as it sniffs out ants and termites among fallen leaves.

**Pyrenean desman**  The cold mountain streams of northern Spain are home to this mammal. The desman swims by wagging its tail and kicking water behind it. It breathes through its long, rubbery snout, which it pokes out of the water like a snorkel. This sensitive snout also helps it to find its food — insects, snails, and worms. Desmans have been heavily hunted and trapped for their thick, soft fur.
***Threatened Species***

**Hedgehog**  Hairs that have evolved into sharp spines protect this rather large insectivore from foxes and other enemies. A threatened hedgehog curls up in a prickly ball that few can attack. From dusk to dawn, hedgehogs sniff their way through woods and gardens, swallowing slugs, beetles, snails, and even snakes. More than a dozen species live in Europe, Africa, and Asia. Where winters are cold, they hibernate.

**Mole**  The common mole, about 6 inches long, is a living digging machine. Its big spade-shaped front feet can burrow long tunnels through soil in just an hour. The plump, velvety mole patrols its tunnels continually and snaps up any earthworms that have fallen in. The mole is almost blind, but its keen senses of smell and touch help it find prey under-ground.

# INSECTIVORES

**Giant otter shrew**  Despite its name, the giant otter shrew is neither an otter nor a shrew. It is related to the hedgehog-like tenrecs of Madagascar. One of the largest insectivores, its body is shaped like an otter's. It catches crabs, fish, and other aquatic creatures in Central African forest streams and swamps.

**Lesser hedgehog tenrec**  This spiny creature looks and behaves like a small European hedgehog. If threatened, it can curl up into a prickly ball. It hibernates in winter, like the European hedgehog, but the two animals are not related. The tenrec can climb trees and lives only in a dry, scrubby region of Madagascar.

**Cape golden mole**  Dense fur that gleams like gold gives this small, blind digger its name. It pushes through sandy soil with its nose, which is protected by a horny shield, and flings loose soil backward with its spadelike front feet. Golden moles are found only in southern Africa. Cape golden moles are native to South Africa's Cape Province.

**Streaked tenrec**  Barbed quills on its back are the main defense of this small creature, which lives in hot, humid Madagascan forests. If threatened by a mongoose, the tenrec can point its quills forward, like a forest of spears, and thrust them into the face or feet of its enemy. Streaked tenrecs burrow for worms in damp, leafy soil.

**Star-nosed mole**  This mole of eastern North America is the only mammal with a ring of tentacles around its snout. The 22 pink feelers probe for food as the mole explores the bottom of a pool or stream. Star-nosed moles are good divers and swimmers and hunt for worms, insects, shellfish, and fish in the water. On land they tunnel in damp soil.

**Moonrat**  The slim, cat-sized moonrat lives in the forests of southeastern Asia. It is heavier than its near relative, the European hedgehog, and instead of being sharp and spiny, its coat is soft, with long, coarse hairs growing untidily through it. Its scaly tail is long and bald, like a rat's. Moonrats can be mostly black or all white. They smell like onions.

# Colugos

Flying lemurs are not lemurs, and they cannot fly! Also called colugos, they have lemur-like faces, but their teeth are more like those of an insectivore. Bats and insectivores seem to be their closest relatives. Flying lemurs actually glide from tree to tree, parachuting on webs of stretched skin. There are only two species, and both live high up in the mountains of southeastern Asia.

**Malayan flying lemur** This cat-sized colugo is one of the best mammal gliders. It can glide more than 400 feet from tree to tree and land only 30 or 40 feet lower than the branch from which it took off. By day it clings to a tree trunk. The flying lemur is active mainly at night, when it eats buds, leaves, and flowers.

# Bats

Bats are the only mammals that can truly fly. Their wings are webs of tough skin stretched between the bones of the hands and the legs.

The nearly 1,000 species of bats can be divided into two broad groups. Fruit bats are larger in size, with big eyes and an appetite for fruit. Most other species are smaller and are insect-eaters. Many have faces and ears shaped to help the bats hear in the dark. They listen for the echoes of their calls, which are bounced off insects or other prey.

**Flying fox** Large eyes and a pointed head and ears make this bat look like a fox. More than 60 species of flying foxes live on lands around the Indian and western Pacific oceans. The world's largest bat is a flying fox: more than 5 feet from wing tip to wing tip. Flocks of flying foxes hang from trees by day. At sunset, they fly off in search of bananas, guavas, papayas, and other fruits or flowers.

**Vampire bat** At night, this mouse-sized bat feeds on blood from living animals. It lands on the ground, then hops or crawls up to its victim and bites it so that the blood flows. The bat's saliva prevents the blood from clotting while the bat is feeding. Although victims lose little blood, they might catch rabies or other diseases transmitted by bat saliva. Vampire bats live in forests from Mexico to South America.

BATS

**Red bat** Bright red fur earns this bat of North and South America its name. The red bat is one of the hardiest of all bat species. In autumn, individuals fly hundreds of miles south from Canada, but many spend the winter in Ohio, where the temperature can fall to less than −10 degrees F. Here these creatures hibernate in tree hollows or rock crevices, with their furry tails wrapped around them and only their noses, wing tips, and ears exposed. Curled up like furry balls, the bats grow sluggish as the temperature falls. Their hearts may beat only 10 times a minute.

**Mexican fishing bat** This New World bat is also called the "bulldog bat" because of its squarish, jowled face and a head that resembles a bulldog's. It skims slowly over water, its tail lifted high in the air. All the time it makes high-pitched squeaks and picks up the echoes sent back from ripples made by fish swimming near the surface. When it detects a fish, the bat lowers its large, clawed feet into the water. They dig into the fish and snatch it up. The bat eats while it is flying, or later, when it lands.

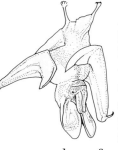

**African yellow-winged bat** Bluish fur and bright orange or yellow wings and ears make this one of the most colorful of all the bats. Its tall, pointed "nose leaf" is thought to help direct the pulses of sound sent out as it flies. A pair of enormous ears detect the echoes bounced back off nearby plants or other objects. Yellow-winged bats live in the open woods in parts of Africa. By day they sleep together in trees, covering their faces with their wings made of skin. At night they snatch up insects from the ground and fly to their roosts to feed.

**Pipistrelle bat** Each autumn male pipistrelles come together and set up roosts in hollow trees. The females arrive later, then mate with a selected few of the males. Males and females hibernate together, but in the spring the males fly off while the females stay together in hollow trees and give birth. On hot summer days you may hear them squeaking noisily. These bats live in many parts of the world.

**Long-eared bat** This bat has long ears with special flaps that might help it find the moths that are its prey. Moths sometimes produce high-pitched clicks to jam the bat's sound-detection system. The bat may outwit the moth by making extra-high or extra-low sounds. Long-eared bats flutter slowly through the trees, sometimes hovering to pluck an insect off a leaf. They roost with their long ears folded back. The brown long-eared bat is found from western Europe to Japan. The gray long-eared bat is found in Europe, North Africa, and Asia.

**Hoary bat** This bat's furry body appears to be covered in sparkling frost, the effect coming from white and white-tipped hairs mingled with dark brown hairs. Its face and throat are a yellowish color. The hoary bat is eastern North America's biggest bat and the only kind native to Hawaii. Long ago, some may have been blown across the Pacific to Hawaii; a few have also crossed the Atlantic that way. Hoary bats regularly migrate to warmer regions in winter. Large groups sometimes fly together like migrating birds, and along the same routes as birds. Like birds, too, a few collide with skyscrapers or other tall structures during their migration flights.

**Horse bat/ hammer-headed bat** Male hammerheaded bats have a long head shaped somewhat like a horse's, which earns them their other name. But their lips are fleshy and their muzzle is wrinkled. With their high voice box, they can make loud honking and croaking noises to attract a mate. Before mating, dozens of males spread out in trees, "sing" and beat their wings. If a female hovers in front of a male, the male flaps his wings faster and speeds up his song into a buzz. Hammerheaded bats live in West and Central Africa. Although they are grouped with fruit-eating bats, they have been seen feeding on dead birds and even attacking chickens in coops.

**Lesser horseshoe bat** Unlike most other bats, this species produces its ultrasonic sounds through its nose, not its mouth. Fleshy horseshoe-shaped lobes around its nose seem to form a kind of megaphone that sends the sound in particular directions. Lesser horseshoe bats and more than 50 other kinds of horseshoe bat live in Europe, North Africa, and Asia.

**Spotted bat** Few bats are as strikingly colored as this small, delicate creature. White spots mark its black or red fur, and its wings and enormous ears are pale pink. Spotted bats are at home among the rocky cliffs and canyons in the deserts of the southwestern United States. They live anywhere, from below sea level to mountains 7,000 feet high. For a long time after scientists discovered spotted bats, people thought the species was rare because so few were seen. They also thought these bats flew only after midnight. Radar and other ultrasonic devices have proved both notions wrong. Spotted bats do fly in the early evening and they are not as rare as people once thought.

# Primates, 1

Primates include humans, apes, monkeys, and their primitive relatives, the prosimians. Primates evolved as tree-climbers, with hands, forward-facing eyes, and a big brain. In time, apes and monkeys drove the prosimians, like the ones shown on these two pages, from most of their forest homes. Now they live mostly on islands. In other, less isolated places, they come out only at night.

These two pages look at three kinds of primates: lorises and pottos, bush babies (galagos), and tarsiers. Lemurs are discussed a little later.

**Needle-clawed bush baby** With its small body, large head, and huge eyes, this is one of the most cuddly-looking of all the bush babies. Many mammals have either claws or nails, but this species has both. A raised ridge runs down each fingernail and sticks out beyond as a sharp claw. The nails protect the sensitive pads of the fingertips. Using its claws, the animal can easily run up and down a big tree. Needle-clawed bush babies are good jumpers, too. They can leap more than 18 feet from branch to branch.

**Slender loris** Soft grayish fur and a silvery underside, plus long and spindly legs, distinguish this small, tailless primate. At night the slender loris moves slowly among the thin branches of low-growing trees. With its huge eyes, it can see in the dark, and it pounces on snails, insects, lizards, and small birds. As it goes along, it wets its hands and feet to leave scent trails as signals to others. The slender loris lives in the forests of southern India and Sri Lanka.

**Philippine tarsier** Its two huge, orange-tinged eyes set in a small face make this tiny southeastern Asian primate resemble a mythical goblin. Like other tarsiers, it has extremely long ankle, or tarsal, bones and long legs for jumping. To catch insects, it leaps from branch to branch, balancing with a wirelike tail that is longer than its tiny, 6-inch body. Its short, strong arms act as shock absorbers, and it clings to branches with spindly, padded fingers and toes.
*Threatened Species*

**Thick-tailed bush baby**  This bush baby's thick tail has a bushy covering of dense hair. It is the largest of the bush babies — about as big as a rabbit — and so it is also known as the greater bush baby. Its muzzle is long and similar to a dog's, and its ears are large. As it climbs trees at night, it can cock one ear forward and the other backward to listen for the tiniest sounds. The thick-tailed bush baby snaps up insects, small reptiles, and birds and also eats birds' eggs and plants. It lives in the forests and wooded grasslands of Africa.

**Slow loris**  Wherever tropical rainforests still stand in southeastern Asia, you might see the slow loris. About 12 inches long, this plump and cautious primate has short ears and a short tail hidden by its fur. A black stripe runs along its back, and it has dark face markings that may scare enemies into thinking it has huge, staring eyes. Slow lorises really live up to their name. All day they sleep, clinging to a branch. At night they ambush small creatures or creep from branch to branch, eating fruit. They mark their territory with urine.

**Potto**  About 15 inches long, the potto has a round head, a short, broad face, thick fur, and a stumpy tail. It shares West Africa's rainforests with the angwantibo, a close relative. The two species rarely meet, for the potto lives high up in tall trees, climbing as cautiously as a tightrope walker as it searches for insects or tasty gum oozing from the bark. Unable to run away, a potto under attack hunches up so that the enemy can bite only its neck and shoulders. Spikes jutting out protect the neck, and its shoulder blades form a shield.

**Angwantibo**  The angwantibo probably gets its name from an African word meaning "cat." People also call it the "golden potto" because of the golden sheen on its fur. It looks like a potto (see entry this page) but is a bit smaller, has an almost invisible stubby tail, and has no bony spines on its neck. The angwantibo climbs slowly, gripping branches with pincerlike hands and feet. It feeds mainly on insects and fruits in the rainforests of West Africa, where it lives.

**Tree shrews**
With its long, furry tail, a scampering tree shrew could be mistaken for a tiny tree squirrel. Like the agile squirrel, many of the 19 species of tree shrews are expert climbers. Balancing with their tails, they run along branches, looking for fruits and insects to eat. They have small, sharp teeth and five claws on each paw. They eat sitting up, holding food in their hands. Most of these lively little mammals live in pairs. They mark their territory with scent to warn off other tree shrews. Their homes are the tropical forests of India and southeastern Asia. Scientists once thought tree shrews should be classified as insectivores. Their faces are certainly long and pointed, like a shrew's, but their brains are bigger and their eyes are larger allowing them to see better. Tree shrews are a little like primitive primates, but scientists class them separately. They probably most strongly resemble the first placental mammals from the Age of Dinosaurs.

**Lesser bush baby**  Much livelier and smaller than its big relative, the thick-tailed bush baby, the lesser bush baby measures no more than 8 inches long. Yet it makes big leaps from tree to tree and can jump more than 6 feet high. Now and then it hops around on the ground like a tiny kangaroo. Among its favorite foods are large insects, which it grabs with its hands as they fly past. At night lesser bush babies hunt alone or in pairs, but family groups sleep together during the daytime. Lesser bush babies live in the open woodlands of Africa.

# Primates, 2

*Lemur* is the Latin word for "ghosts". Lemurs got that name because they travel unseen through the trees at night. Some also make weird sounds. Lemurs are primitive primates (prosimians). They have long and pointed muzzles, staring eyes, and a dense coat of woolly hair. Their jutting front teeth can strip bark from trees or skin from fruit, and their thumbs and toes are good at gripping branches. Most lemurs climb on all fours, but the so-called leaping lemurs run and jump upright, like humans. When true monkeys appeared, about 25 million years ago, they drove out the lemurs. Today some 16 kinds survive only on Madagascar and nearby islands.

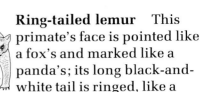

**Ring-tailed lemur**   This primate's face is pointed like a fox's and marked like a panda's; its long black-and-white tail is ringed, like a raccoon's. Walking on all fours, it resembles a long-legged cat. Sometimes a male starts a stink fight. He smears his tail with smelly secretions from glands on his chest and waves his tail over his head. This usually scares off other males.
*Threatened Species*

**Indri**   *"Indri"* cried the guide on the island of Madagascar, pointing to an animal with yellow eyes, black-and-white fur, and a stumpy tail. *Indri* is the Malagasy word for "look," but a European explorer mistook it for the animal's name. These leaping lemurs look human as they sit in a tree, dangling their long legs. They leap from tree trunk to tree trunk to feed on leaves. Groups of indris bark and howl in chorus to advertise their forest territory.
*Threatened Species*

**Aye-aye**   Like the woodpecker, the aye-aye from Madagascar feeds on insects living in old wood. It does not peck holes but uses its immensely long, flexible middle finger to coax wood-boring grubs from the holes or to scrape food from the holes it bites out of coconuts. This rare nocturnal creature has staring eyes, a catlike face, pointed ears, and a coat of coarse hair covering its body. It also has a very long, bushy tail.
*Threatened Species*

**Verreaux's sifaka**   This primate moves in huge leaps, taking off and landing on its springy hind legs, which are longer than its arms. It jumps and lands upright, like an indri, but has a long tail that is usually carried curled up. It eats leaves, flowers, and fruit.
*Threatened Species*

**Black lemur**   All black lemurs are born black. The males stay black, but after six months the females become reddish brown. A group of black lemurs claims a patch of forest by marking objects with scent rubbed off their front limbs and by producing terrifying shrieks.
*Threatened Species*

**Coquerel's mouse lemur**   With a head and body as long as a human forearm, Coquerel's mouse lemur is a giant compared to its relative, the lesser mouse lemur, which could quite easily fit in someone's hand. As they climb about in branches, Coquerel's mouse lemurs give off a strong odor. This informs other Coquerel mouse lemurs of their presence. The dry forests of western Madagascar are the only places where these shy creatures can be found.
*Threatened Species*

**Ruffed lemur**   This largest of the lemurs has a long ruff around its neck. Of the four color variations, the black-and-white kind shown here is probably the most handsome. Ruffed lemurs forage for tree bark, fruits, and leaves. Nimble climbers, they seldom come down out of the trees. They may bark like a dog, neigh like a horse, or cluck like a hen.
*Threatened Species*

# Primates, 3

More than 50 kinds of monkeys live in the hot, humid forests of Central and South America. The nostrils of these New World monkeys are wide apart and flare outward. Scientists call these monkeys *platyrrhines*, meaning "flat noses." Many have a long tail that is as good as a hand for grasping branches. Because they cannot press their thumb and other fingers together, their hands are not very useful for that. New World monkeys tend to have thick, woolly fur. One family group consists of capuchin monkeys, howler monkeys, ouakaris, sakis, spider monkeys, squirrel monkeys, and woolly monkeys. Another contains the marmosets and tamarins. Some of these are as small as mice; none is bigger than a squirrel.

**Red howler monkey** This large South American forest species is unquestionably one of the noisiest creatures in the world. You can hear a male red howler calling from 2 miles away as he warns rivals to keep off his territory. What makes the sound so loud is an extra-large voice box with a hollow bone that acts as a sounding board.

**Black-capped or brown capuchin** These are popular pets because of their lively curiosity. In the forest they search every nook and cranny for insects; they also munch on flowers, shoots, and fruits. As they move from tree to tree, capuchins unintentionally pollinate forest flowers; one group's droppings can spread 300,000 tiny seeds in a single day.

**Black spider monkey** No South American monkey is more agile than this long-limbed, long-tailed forest acrobat. A spider monkey swings through branches by its arms and hangs upside down by its tail to pluck fruit. Bare skin near its tip keeps the tail firmly coiled around a branch.
***Threatened Species***

**White-faced saki** Sakis are small, flat-faced South American monkeys with a coarse, thick coat. The white-faced saki gets its name from its distinctive face markings. The male white-faced saki has a white or yellowish fringe of fur around the face and a black body and tail. The female is brown, speckled with gray. Sakis usually walk slowly along a branch on all fours, but a saki in a hurry bounds along. It hops from branch to branch like a kangaroo and takes flying leaps.

**Bald ouakari** Its bald and bright red head and face make this shaggy-coated monkey resemble a tiny old man in a long fur coat. Because of its long fur, the ouakari appears bigger than it really is. An excited ouakari makes its fur stand on end so that it appears even larger. Ouakaris live in forests that flood when the Amazon River overflows.
***Threatened Species***

**Common squirrel monkey** This is a slim, long-tailed monkey with a short coat and attractive markings. Its white face and ears contrast handsomely with its dark eyes, crown, and mouth. Squirrel monkeys run nimbly along branches as they work their way through the South American forests searching for fruits, nuts, insects, and small birds to eat. As many as 500 squirrel monkeys have been seen together. Humans are the only primates known to form larger crowds.

**Humboldt's woolly monkey** Short, woolly coats give these big South American plant-eaters a cuddly appearance, but males can inflict a nasty bite. Troops of up to 50 crash through a forest, running on all fours along branches or swinging by their arms and tail. As a greeting, they purse their lips and kiss.
***Threatened Species***

**Emperor tamarin**   A long, drooping white mustache identifies this small, agile monkey. It was named after the Austrian emperor Franz Josef, who also had a long mustache. Emperor tamarins can resemble squirrels as they leap and run along tree branches. Small groups make shrill sounds while they hunt for insects, spiders, and other small prey in the hot, humid forests of the western Amazon Basin. Tamarins have longer lower canine teeth than their relatives, the marmosets, and do not chew wood as often.

**Common marmoset**   This marmoset is about the size of a squirrel. Family groups roam the Brazilian forests, sucking sap and gum from holes gnawed in trees. The female usually has twins, which the male carries on his back, passing them to the mother at feeding time.

**Golden lion tamarin**   This is one of the most beautiful but rarest South American monkeys. Long, silky, golden hair covers its head and shoulders like a lion's mane. Golden lion tamarins became scarce as Brazil's southeastern forests disappeared, leaving only patches for them to live in. Zoos began breeding the monkeys to save them and are now releasing some of the young back into the wild.

***Threatened Species***

**Pygmy marmoset**   The pygmy marmoset is one of the world's smallest monkeys. Three together may weigh no more than a hamster. In the forests of the western Amazon Basin, they creep and scuttle through the trees, making high-pitched sounds like those of song-birds. They search for fruits and insects but spend even more time clinging upright to trees, gnawing holes in the bark and then sucking the gum or sap that slowly oozes out. Brown fur flecked with light hair hides them in the forest.

**Silvery marmoset**   The silvery marmoset, though small, is striking in appearance, with its bare, reddish face and ears, black tail, and silky white body fur. Small groups live in the tropical forests of Bolivia and Brazil, scampering through the trees and shrubs. Silvery marmosets warn rivals by raising their eyebrows.

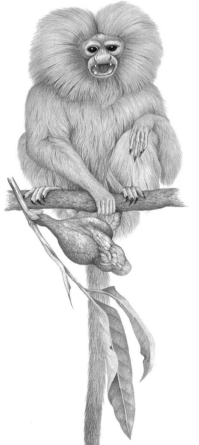

**Goeldi's marmoset**   This small, dark monkey has a long mane of hair. It searches for food in the trees and may come down to the ground if startled by a bird of prey. It may be rare now due to the disappearance of so many forests in the Amazon Basin.

# Primates, 4

Most of the world's monkeys live in the hot, forested regions of two Old World continents: Africa and Asia. The nostrils of Old World monkeys are set close together and face downward, and so scientists call these monkeys *catarrhines*, meaning "down-facing noses." Most Old World monkeys have a good hand grip but cannot grasp branches with their tails. Some have hardly any tail at all. All Old World monkeys can sit without becoming sore, thanks to tough pads of skin on their bare buttocks.

**Allen's swamp monkey**    The swampy forests of Central Africa are home to this little-known monkey, which lives in groups. Although it eats mainly fruits and other plant foods, it also goes into the water to catch crabs and fish.

**Patas monkey**    Caution and long sprinter's legs help this African species survive on open grasslands. Each group has a male "lookout" that goes on ahead and climbs trees to scout for danger. If the monkeys are chased, they can dash off at more than 30 miles an hour.

**Barbary ape**    This is not a true ape but a macaque monkey with hardly any tail. The barbary ape roams the northwestern African mountains. Those brought years ago to the Rock of Gibraltar are the only wild monkeys now living in Europe. ***Threatened Species***

**Talapoin**    This is one of the smallest African monkeys — less than 15 inches long, not counting the tail. Troops of up to 20 live in mangrove swamps and other wet forests in West Africa. Talapoins are good swimmers. They eat water plants and steal cassavas and other root crops grown in pools.

**Japanese macaque**    This monkey lives farther north than does any other monkey. Thick fur keeps it warm on northern Honshu Island, where the snowfall is heavy in winter and there is only bark to eat. Some Japanese macaques bathe in the island's hot springs in winter.

**White-cheeked mangabey**    Long tufts of hair on the eyebrows and a flowing mane help distinguish this relative of the baboons. The mangabey's enormously long tail grips the branches to help the animal move around. Mangabey monkeys rip off bark to chew it or to uncover insects hiding beneath. Any food left over is stuffed into cheek pouches to eat later. A group wandering through an African forest makes loud "whoop-gobble" calls to warn off other groups.

### Mustached monkey

Among the small-to-medium-sized long-tailed monkeys known as "guenons," none has a more colorful head than this. The bare skin on its face is blue. The furry cheeks are yellow. Below the nose is a curved white stripe. Below this, black hairs form a fringe that looks like a mustache. Such striking markings help monkeys recognize each other when several similar species live in the same area. Mustached monkeys are found in the forests of Central Africa.

### Black-and-white colobus monkey

Colobus monkeys have no thumbs; in fact, their name comes from a Greek word meaning "maimed." Black-and-white colobus monkeys are born white but within six months begin to develop the black coloring. Adults are attractive, with long, silky white hair trailing from their sides and tail. Many of these African leaf-eaters are heavier than a small dog, yet are amazing treetop acrobats. Families move silently through the forest, making huge leaps and sometimes landing on thin branches.

### Mandrill
A male mandrill weighs as much as a young teenager. It has a huge muzzle, with blue skin on both sides of a long scarlet nose. The male's rump is hairless and also brightly colored, with just a short, stumpy tail. Perhaps this helps males attract the smaller, duller females. These heavy monkeys roam forest clearings in West Africa, feeding on fruits, insects, and small mammals and raiding crops.
***Threatened Species***

**Diana monkey**    With its black face, white chest and thigh stripe, and chestnut back, this guenon is one of the most striking monkeys in all Africa. Diana monkeys come in two varieties: long-bearded and short-bearded. Unfortunately, both are becoming rare in West Africa's steadily shrinking forests. These lively climbers feed on fruits among the branches of the tallest trees. Up there the Diana does not have to compete with others feeding lower down.
*Threatened Species*

**Gelada**    Geladas look quite different from other baboons. They have hollow cheeks and small nostrils set far back. The chest contains bare red patches, and a long, thick mane runs halfway down the male's back. Geladas live in the wild mountain regions of Ethiopia. Each group contains a full-grown male with his wives and children, but several hundred geladas may roam about together. By day they wander over mountain meadows, eating roots, grasses, and small animals.  At night, geladas climb to ledges on steep cliffs, where they are relatively safe from predators.

**Olive colobus monkey**    West Africa's olive colobus is much smaller than its black-and-white relative and has shorter hair. People know less about this species, partly because of its gray-green fur, which makes the monkey difficult to see in the gloomy undergrowth of the forest. Family groups eat leaves on low tree branches and sleep higher up, but they seldom visit treetops or the ground. The species is very rare.

**Hanuman langur**    This is a large, slim, leaf-eating monkey with heavy eyebrows, long arms, and hands with five fingers and short thumbs. Hanuman langurs live in or near India. They can climb well but spend much of their time on the ground. Up to 25 or more will raid a garden or an orchard. India's Hindus let them do this, believing that the animals are holy.

**Olive baboon**    Baboons are large, ground-dwelling monkeys found in Africa and Arabia. Olive baboons have a doglike face and long, sharp teeth. Troops of up to 150 roam the open grasslands of Africa, eating plants, insects, lizards, and even young antelopes. The baby clings to its mother's belly until it is about a month old. Then it moves to the mother's back.

**Proboscis monkey**    The male's amazingly long nose, or proboscis, explains how this monkey got its name. (The female's nose is much smaller and turns up, not down.) The male's nose helps give the monkey's loud, honking cry its special sound. Males can become quite heavy, with a belly that bulges from their having eaten many mangrove leaves, yet they climb and leap through the trees of Borneo's mangrove swamps with ease. Proboscis monkeys are good swimmers, too.
*Threatened Species*

# Primates, 5

Apes, our closest living relatives, split off long ago from monkeys. The faces of these large, tailless primates are more human-looking than are those of monkeys. In addition, apes tend to hold their bodies more upright. Most can hang and swing from branches by their long arms. Apes are big-brained and live long lives. They grow up more slowly than monkeys and so have extra time to learn how to find food and avoid danger in the forest.

The lightly built gibbons swing fastest through the trees. Orangutans also spend a lot of time high up in the branches. Chimpanzees and gorillas find much of their food on the ground.

**Siamang** The siamang of Malaysia and Sumatra is the largest of the gibbons — a black ape weighing about 25 pounds. Siamangs swing nimbly through the trees and balance themselves perfectly as they stroll along a branch, arms held above their head. They even sleep high off the ground. These gibbons live in family groups and communicate by shrill whooping barks that make their throats bulge like balloons.

**Hoolock gibbon** Hoolock gibbons are born light-colored but soon turn black (males) or brown (females). Adults weigh only about 15 pounds. These gibbons live from eastern India to Myanmar and South China but are becoming scarce.
***Threatened Species***

**White-handed gibbon** Other names for this small, acrobatic ape include the agile, lar, silvery, and common gibbon. White-handed gibbons run on two feet along branches and swing from tree to tree at top speed, grasping first with one hand, then the other, to leap gaps of 40 feet at a time. Now and then a female's clear hooting call can be heard getting louder and louder, then trailing off as if she is sad. Each group travels about 1 mile a day searching for fruit to eat in the forests of Thailand and Malaysia.

**Gorilla** No other primate is as large and as heavy as this black ape of the forests of West and Central Africa. Males weigh up to 450 pounds; females are much smaller. Females and their young often climb trees, but males usually stay on the ground. They stand and walk resting on their knuckles. Despite their size, gorillas lead very peaceful lives, munching on juicy plants and dozing in nests of leaves and twigs. Each group has a leader, a "silverback," which is an older male with a silvery-gray back.
***Threatened Species***

**Orangutan** "Man of the forest" is what this mammal's name means. With its flat face and reddish beard, Asia's only great ape does look somewhat human, though the males weigh more than most men do. Orangutans can amble on all fours, using their long arms as legs, but they prefer climbing slowly from tree to tree, grasping branches with feet that grip like hands. Adults come together to mate or to share fruit on a tree. Orangutans live only in Borneo and Sumatra.
***Threatened Species***

**Chimpanzee** This African forest ape is an intelligent user of tools. Some chimpanzees will eat termites they catch by poking twigs into nests. They may open nuts by smashing them with stones, or drink water mopped up with a leaf used as a sponge. Chimpanzees live in groups and communicate using special sounds and gestures. A group may even band together to catch and kill a monkey for food, although plants make up most of their diet. Chimpanzees are good climbers but spend most of the day on the ground.
***Threatened Species***

# Carnivores, 1

The pages in this section describe the meat-eating mammals, or carnivores. Most have sharp teeth and claws to catch and kill other animals for food. Some carnivores, such as the big cats, can even kill animals larger than themselves. The biggest carnivore of all is the polar bear; the smallest is a weasel. Besides cats, bears, and weasels, carnivore families include dogs, raccoons, civets and mongooses, walruses, hyenas, and both eared and earless seals.

This page shows all 4 species in the hyena family. The next page shows 6 of the roughly 30 kinds of mongooses. Most hyenas are doglike hunters and scavengers, with big heads and powerful jaws. Mongooses, much smaller than hyenas, have long, slim bodies and short legs. Some have been known to attack and kill poisonous snakes.

Hyenas and mongooses live in Africa and Asia. Their closest relatives are probably the civets.

**Aardwolf**   People sometimes shoot aardwolves, believing them to be hyenas. However, they are smaller and have five, not four, toes on their front feet. Aardwolves live on the African plains in holes in the ground. That is how they got their name, which means "earth wolf." They eat mainly termites.

**Spotted hyena**   A little smaller than the big cats, the spotted hyena is as heavy as an adult human. It is a formidable hunter. Whoops, yells, and cackles explain its other name of laughing hyena. These sounds help a pack of hyenas keep in touch while scouring the African plains for food, alive or dead. A pack will drive a lion from its kill, and a lone hyena can bring down a wildebeest of more than twice its own weight.

**Striped hyena**   Striped hyenas are smaller than spotted hyenas. They hide in dens by day and come out at night, alone or in pairs, to hunt. These animals are chiefly scavengers, but they will pursue small, live prey such as mice and lizards. They have even been known to kill dogs and sheep. Striped hyenas live in thorny and stony parts of northern and eastern Africa, southwestern Asia, and India.

**Brown hyena**   A mane of long hair hangs from the brown hyena's neck and shoulders. Its diet is varied. It may steal ostrich eggs, eat whales that have been washed ashore, or even drive a leopard from its kill. A mother moves her three-month-old cubs to a nursery den, where other females help feed them.
***Threatened Species***

**Ring-tailed mongoose** Only two kinds of mongoose are good tree climbers, and this is one. Ring-tailed mongooses scamper up trees to catch insects, birds, lizards, and small mammals. They quickly get down again if taken by surprise. This species is one of several Madagascan mongooses.

**Cusimanse** Cusimanses are West African mongooses with long, twitchy noses. Family groups chatter as they sniff the ground, digging up worms and insects or catching crabs, frogs, or small birds and mammals. Eggs are the cusimanses' favorite food. To break the shells, they pick up the eggs and hurl them at trees or rocks.

**Banded mongoose** Most small carnivores live alone, but banded mongooses live in packs inside holes bored into termite mounds. While one male stays at home to care for the young, the rest go off to hunt for beetles. These African mongooses will gang up to drive off an attacking jackal. Some were once seen rescuing a mongoose that had been seized by an eagle.

**Meerkat** Black-ringed eyes make meerkats (or suricates) look like bandits. Up to 30 of these small mongooses live together. One will stand guard on its hind legs while others dig for scorpions and beetles. At a cry of warning all scamper down the same burrow to safety.

**Small Indian mongoose** This little Asian carnivore proved so effective at killing rats and snakes that the species was introduced to the Caribbean and Hawaiian islands, where rats had damaged whole crops of sugarcane. The mongooses killed many of the rats, but they also showed a taste for chickens and rare island birds and lizards. Now the islanders treat them as pests, but they continue to thrive.

**Marsh mongoose** Of all the mongooses, this may be the best swimmer and diver. It lives in Africa along marshes and rivers, catching crabs, fish, and frogs. Very large for a mongoose, it is about as heavy as a small dog.

# Carnivores, 2

The dog family includes, besides domesticated dogs, wolves, foxes, coyotes, jackals, and wild dogs. There are about 35 wild species altogether. The largest is the gray wolf, or timber wolf. A big wolf can weigh as much as a man. The smallest species is the fennec fox, which is about the size of a rabbit.

Dogs first appeared in North America. Most species have evolved for chasing prey across open countryside. Dogs walk and run on their toes. They have strong jaws, a muscular body, and a bushy tail.

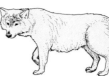

**Gray wolf** The ancestor of domesticated dogs, the gray or timber wolf is the largest and strongest member of the dog family. Gray wolves are found in northern North America, Asia, and northern Europe. Killing by humans, though, has reduced their numbers. Wolves hunt in packs of up to 15 strong. The packs are led by a male and a female. Individuals in a pack work together as a team to trick or run down prey that may range in size from beavers to caribou. One wolf might show itself to rouse the curiosity of its prey while others in the pack creep up unobserved. The other wolves then rush in to make the kill. A caribou hunt can involve a long chase. The pack may follow the caribou for many miles at an easy, loping run. When an old or sick deer falls behind, the wolves close in and kill it with their strong, sharp teeth. The pack leaders always get the choicest parts of the animals to eat.
***Threatened Species***

**Black-backed jackal** A black back distinguishes this handsome, foxlike hunter-scavenger. Black-backed jackals roam the plains over much of Africa. They hunt in pairs and chase or stalk small antelopes, bringing them down and then killing them with a bite to the throat. These jackals will eat almost anything. They are just as content to eat animals they find already dead, and what they cannot eat immediately they bury for eating later. Even where there are plenty of antelopes, the jackals gobble up the dung beetles that live in the antelope droppings. Antelopes and antelope droppings are scarce in the Kalahari Desert, but the jackals survive there by crunching up juicy locusts.

**Red fox**   The red fox is a wild dog that is famous for its cunning. Red foxes are enemies of farmers, who try to shoot, trap, or poison them. Yet the red fox easily survives because it is crafty and can live anywhere and eat whatever food it finds. Few mammals, apart from rats and humans, can adapt as well as red foxes to so many different conditions. They thrive right across the northern hemisphere and also in Australia, where they were released.

**Coyote**   The mournful howl of the coyote is a familiar sound in North America's deserts, prairies, and mountains. Farmers dislike coyotes because they kill lambs and calves, although often the killed lambs were already weak or dying. Coyotes may also steal beans and fruits from farms. However, they are certainly the farmers' friends in one way: they eat rabbits and grass-eating rodents. When farmers kill off coyotes, the smaller animals multiply too fast, robbing the sheep and cattle of nourishment.

**African hunting dog**   A hunting dog is far smaller than a lion, but zebras and large antelopes fear it just as much, for this is the "wolf" of Africa. Hunting in packs, wild dogs are fast, and they are ferocious enough to tackle nearly anything. They will trot toward a zebra or large antelope, then slow down to a walk that changes to a gallop as the animal begins to run. The lead dogs seize the head and tail to slow the prey down while the rest tear into its flesh. Then the whole pack shares the meat.
***Threatened Species***

**Bat-eared fox**   Huge ears are the most noticeable feature of this fox, which weighs about half as much as a red fox. These foxes live in hot, dry parts of eastern and southwestern Africa, and the ears help shed heat. Although these foxes look a bit like short-legged jackals, their teeth are much smaller. However, they are sharp enough to crunch up the insects that are the foxes' main food. A bat-eared fox has more teeth than any other placental mammal except for certain whales.

**Dingo**   When European explorers reached Australia, they found large domestic dogs running wild. These dingoes had probably traveled there in the boats of settlers who had arrived about 3,000 years earlier. Scientists suspect that dingoes helped destroy Australia's Tasmanian devils and thylacines (marsupial "wolves"). They certainly kill cattle, sheep, and kangaroos. Angry farmers have shot and poisoned thousands of dingoes. Still they continue to thrive, but many have interbred with domesticated European dogs.

**Fennec fox**   This carnivore has the smallest body of any fox. Fennecs live in very hot North African and Arabian deserts. Their large ears work like radiators to help them keep cool, and they escape the hottest parts of the day by burrowing. A fennec hunts by night, its sensitive ears catching the slightest sounds made by beetles, scorpions, baby birds, or desert hares. The water in the body of its prey provides the fox with moisture.
***Threatened Species***

**Arctic fox**   The Artic fox is built to withstand cold. Its body is compact, with small ears, a rather short muzzle, short legs, and a very thick white coat. All this helps prevent a loss of body heat. In winter long hairs on the Arctic fox's feet help it walk across fresh snow, and its white coat makes it almost invisible to its enemies. In spring its coat turns darker. The Arctic fox lives on lemmings, Arctic hares, birds, birds' eggs, berries, carcasses, kitchen garbage, and even reindeer droppings.

**Maned wolf**   This animal earns its name from the long hair along its back that forms a raised mane. The maned wolf (in fact a fox) is the second biggest member of the dog family. It has long legs to help it see over tall grasses and to run faster than any of its close relatives. This shy creature lives in south-central South America.
***Threatened Species***

**Gray fox**   Common in most of the United States and ranging into South America, the gray fox is slightly smaller than the red fox and has a black-tipped, not a white-tipped, tail. The gray fox will climb trees, like a cat.

# Carnivores, 3

Bears are large, shaggy carnivores with big heads, powerful jaws, short, strong legs, and broad feet. They usually shuffle along flat-footed but can break into a lumbering gallop. Some kinds climb trees, and the polar bear is an excellent swimmer.

With their heavy claws, most bears can dig up roots, tear open bees' nests, and injure other animals. One swipe of a grizzly's paw could easily kill a deer or a person. But bears have a more varied diet than most other carnivores and will try to avoid conflict, preferring to spend their lives quietly roaming the woods alone. They hear better than they see but rely mostly on their keen sense of smell.

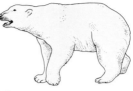

**Polar bear**    This is probably the biggest bear — nearly 11 feet tall and weighing almost a ton. Polar bears are strong swimmers. In their search for seals they will cross wide expanses of water between Arctic Ocean ice floes. They are protected from the cold by thick, ivory-colored fur. On land a polar bear can outrun a caribou.
***Threatened Species***

**Sun bear**    To Eastern peoples, the curved mark on this bear's chest stands for the rising sun. This is the smallest bear, about 3 feet tall. It is also the most agile climber of any bear. During the day it sleeps in treetop nests. At night it hunts for small creatures and wild bees' nests. The sun bear lives in the forests of southeastern Asia.
***Threatened Species***

**Asiatic black bear**    Light markings on the chest distinguish this black bear from the slightly larger American black bear. The Asian species is quite fearless and will kill sheep, goats, ponies, and even people. It lives in forests from Afghanistan across Asia to Japan.
***Threatened Species***

**Sloth bear**    This shaggy bear's name comes from an old belief that the animal was really a sloth. Sloth bears shuffle through the Indian and Sri Lankan forests, using their long claws to tear open termite nests. Pursing its floppy lips into a tube shape, a sloth bear can suck up insects like a vacuum cleaner.
***Threatened Species***

**Brown bear**    This is the largest carnivore of inland Europe and northern Asia. It is shy and quick-tempered. Weighing up to 1,600 pounds, a large male stands over 8 feet tall. In autumn, brown bears eat huge quantities of fruits and berries. Then they go to sleep for the winter in a cave or hollow tree.

**Spectacled bear**    This bear has pale markings resembling glasses around its eyes. The only bear native to South America, it lives in cool forests high in the Andes Mountains. The spectacled bear eats fruits, leaves, and roots and sometimes kills animals as big as deer. Hunting and forest destruction have made this species rare.
***Threatened Species***

**Grizzly bear**    Grizzly and Kodiak bears are the North American varieties of the brown bear, which is also found in Asia and Europe. Alaskan grizzly bears are among the largest carnivores to live on land. They use their powerful claws to dig for mice and ground squirrels, and some scoop salmon from rivers. A grizzly bear that feels threatened can be extremely dangerous.

**American black bear**    As many as 75,000 black bears inhabit North American forests. They stand about 5 feet tall, weigh more than an average person, and can run fast and climb trees. Black bears eat anything from berries, honey, and insects to small mammals. Some will beg for food at campsites.

# Carnivores, 4

Raccoons and pandas seem closely related. It is most likely that they evolved from the same prehistoric carnivores that gave rise to dogs and bears. Some scientists think giant pandas *are* bears.

Besides the raccoons themselves, the raccoon family includes the coati, kinkajou, olingo, and more than half a dozen other species. Like raccoons, these animals live in the Americas and are lively, wiry creatures that are at home climbing trees. Although they are carnivores, the kinkajou and the olingo eat a lot of fruit. Pandas behave even less like carnivores. Asia's giant panda and red panda both enjoy munching on the tall, dry grass called bamboo.

**Red panda** With its long, bushy tail, this rust-colored animal about 3 feet long resembles the raccoon more than the giant panda. However, both pandas are the only carnivores to eat a great deal of bamboo, and both have the same unusual kind of wristbone. Red pandas spend the day curled up asleep in trees and move about to feed at night. If one is startled, it will hiss and spit like a cat. Red pandas live in mountain forests from Nepal to southwestern China; they may be endangered.

**Raccoon** An appealing face, handlike paws, and a bushy tail make the 3-foot-long "coon" one of North America's favorite backyard animals. Once all raccoons lived in the woods. However, when people cut down the trees, raccoons began appearing in towns. Many now raid garbage cans, looking like small, furry bandits in black masks. In captivity they dip food in water before eating it. This may be because they are used to catching water animals to eat in the wild.

**Olingo** About the same length as a raccoon but lighter and more agile, the olingo lives high up in the treetops in the lush forests of Central America and northern South America. At night, balancing on a long tail, they scamper nimbly along branches and leap from tree to tree. They almost never come down to the ground. Sometimes a group will form and maybe even join a group of relatives, the kinkajous, to search for fruit. The olingo also eats insects, birds, and small mammals.

**Giant panda** This big, bearlike mammal is familiar to many of us as the symbol of the World Wildlife Fund. Fewer than 1,000 of these endangered creatures may be left, and the species could soon become extinct. Giant pandas lead very isolated lives, roaming forested mountains in southwestern China and eastern Tibet. They eat bamboo, grabbing shoots with thumblike pads on their front feet.
***Threatened Species***

**Coati** This relative of the North American raccoon is found mainly in South America. The coati has short legs, a long, ringed tail, and a long snout. Coatis are lively and intelligent. Bands made up of 30 or more females and their young bound through forests carrying their tails high, like flags. They sniff logs and holes and scratch to find small animals to eat. Coatis can kill lizards with a quick bite but will crush some creatures between their paws, perhaps to crack a shell or to rub away the pain of a sting.

**Kinkajou** The kinkajou is one of only two carnivores that have a tail that can grip like an extra hand. Kinkajous are agile climbers. They scamper through treetops but do not leap, as monkeys do. Sometimes a kinkajou will wrap its tail around a branch and hang upside down, leaving its hands free to grab a tasty fruit. Its long tongue is good at scooping pulp from soft tropical fruits, lapping up nectar from flowers, and catching insects. Kinkajous are forest dwellers and are found in Central and South America.

**The "honey bear"**
Sometimes animals are given funny nicknames. The kinkajou (described on the left) is also known as the "honey bear." The kinkajou loves sweet things to eat and will lap up honey from bees' nests. Kinkajous are tame and friendly and can be kept as pets. They only bite if they are roughly handled.

# Carnivores, 5

Civets and genets are medium-sized, catlike animals with long bodies, long tails, and short legs. They belong to the animal family that some zoologists think should include mongooses.

Civets look and behave much like wildcats. Their name comes from an Arabic word for the scents used by civets for marking territory. Civets live in Africa and southeastern Asia.

There are about 10 kinds of genets. Genets are medium-sized carnivores with rows of dark spots or stripes, long, ringed tails, and claws that can be drawn in, like a cat's. Secretive and most active at night, they live in Africa, southwestern Asia, and southwestern Europe.

**Small-spotted genet** This lightly built carnivore is about 3 feet long. Its head is small and its body slim. Rows of dark spots run down its back and sides, and black rings encircle its long tail. The small-spotted genet creeps up on rodents or other small animals, crouches like a cat, then pounces. It is an agile climber and kills birds roosting in trees. It is native to southwestern Europe, Africa, and parts of southwestern Asia. In these regions, people sometimes keep genets as pets, to kill mice and rats.

**Giant genet** In 1911 the skin of an unknown animal reached London. It resembled that of a small-spotted genet but was larger and more heavily marked. Someone had sent it from near Lake Victoria in East Africa, so scientists assumed that was where the creature lived. They named it *Genetta victoriae*, or Lake Victoria genet. Years later, scientists discovered that this little-known carnivore lives mainly in forests far to the west of the lake. As a result, the scientific name of the giant genet is misleading.

**Masked palm civet** A black-and-white face striped like a badger's and a plain gray-brown tail and body make this civet easy to identify. When night falls, it scampers up trees and along the ground searching for food. It eats fruits and roots and catches insects, lizards, rats, and mice. Any animal attacking it gets a shock, for the civet turns its back and sprays its enemy with a foul-smelling fluid from scent glands beneath its tail. The masked palm civet lives in Asia — from the island of Borneo to the Himalayas.

**African civet** This powerfully built civet has a broad head and

thick neck, much like a dog's. One of the largest civets, it weighs about 45 pounds and measures 4 feet, not counting its tail. Although it can climb trees, it hunts mainly on the ground and often sleeps in caves or aardvark burrows. Before synthetic perfumes were invented, people made perfume with the strong-smelling musk produced by glands near the civet's tail. These creatures live throughout Africa.

**The Fossa**
Madagascar's largest carnivore is a slim, catlike mammal up to 5 feet long. Scientists classify it as a civet, yet civets have 36 teeth, while the fossa has only 32. Although it can pull in its claws like a cat, it walks flat-footed, like a bear. It must have had the same ancestors as cats and civets. On Madagascar it takes the place of cats, which never got to the island. Hunting at night, fossas chase lemurs up trees and attack chickens and even pigs.

**Sulawesi palm civet** The Sulawesi palm civet gets its name from the Indonesian island of Sulawesi, where it lives. It is equally at home in low-lying forests, mountain forests, and on land with just a covering of scrub. Brown and about 5 feet long, it feeds largely on fruits and mice. Although not yet extinct, as was once feared, this species *could* disappear if people burn and chop down what remains of Sulawesi's fast-disappearing forests.

# Carnivores, 6

Badgers, martens, otters, skunks, and weasels are all mustelids, or members of the weasel family of carnivores. There are more than 60 kinds, ranging from a weasel lighter than a hamster to the wolverine, as heavy as a large dog. All have long, low bodies, with scent glands near the tail for marking territory. Mustelids can be found all over the world except in Antarctica and Australia and on the island of Madagascar.

**Honey badger** A fondness for honey earned this stockily built animal the name of honey badger. In Africa it satisfies its taste for honey with help from a small bird called the honey guide. Flying ahead, a honey guide leads a honey badger to a bees' nest, which the badger rips open with its powerful claws. Then both animals share the prize. Honey badgers live in Africa, the Middle East, and India.

**Eurasian badger** A large family of these badgers shares a maze of linked burrows that have several entrances. The animals spend all day and all winter inside, dozing on a bed of leaves. In warm weather young badgers play outside, and adults drag out bedding now and then to air it. They also dig pits to use as toilets. Their varied diet includes roots, worms, and fruits.

**American badger** The only badger native to America has a heavy, low-slung body similar to but smaller than the Eurasian badger's. It is also more carnivorous, digging fast with powerful claws to root out prairie dogs and any snakes trying to share their holes. It lives on the open plains from southwestern Canada to Mexico.

**Spotted-necked otter** Lakes and rivers south of the Sahara Desert are the habitats of this 3-foot-long streamlined swimmer, which has a spotted chin and throat. An otter family will dive playfully through a lake, catching fish, frogs, and crustaceans. As many as 20 otters might be found together. If a spotted-necked otter becomes anxious, it makes a "ffff" sound. All other kinds of otters make a "hah" sound.

**Chinese ferret-badger** This is one of three ferret-badgers, all from southeastern Asia. The Chinese ferret-badger has light markings on its face and back, a body about the length of a small terrier's, and a tail half its length. It's a good climber and hunts for birds' eggs, insects, lizards, mice, and fruits in trees. If disturbed while asleep in its burrow, it can become savage.

**Eurasian otter** Like all otters, this one is perfectly built for swimming. At the water's surface it paddles with all four webbed feet. To gain speed underwater, it tucks in its legs and wiggles its rear end. The young are born in burrows by streams. European otters are now scarce. However, Asia and North America still have many river otters.

**Sea otter** This otter is well adapted to a life spent in the sea. It has flipperlike hind feet and dense, waterproof fur. Off the rocky North Pacific coast, the sea otter dives to pick up shellfish and stones from the seabed. Floating on its back with a shellfish on its chest, the otter smashes the shell with a stone. Sea otters were once so heavily hunted for their fur that they almost disappeared.

**Patagonian weasel** Not much is known about this small carnivore. Although its chewing teeth are small, its cutting teeth are large and sharp, so it is probably a capable hunter of small mammals and birds. This South American mustelid lives on the windswept grasslands of southern Argentina and Chile.

**Weasel** This smallest of all carnivores has a head and body shorter than a man's foot. The weasel is slim enough to chase a mouse or vole down a narrow hole and agile enough to scamper up a tree to collect birds' eggs and nestlings. Weasels will also kill rabbits. They live in North America, Europe, and Asia.

**Marbled polecat** A marbled pattern on its back makes this mustelid easy to identify. Marbled polecats can grow nearly 3 feet long and are powerful enough to root out ground squirrels and hamsters from their burrows. An angry polecat arches its tail like a skunk and emits a foul smell. The marbled polecat lives on grassy plains from eastern Europe to China.

**Striped skunk**    A skunk's black-and-white markings are not just for show. They tell enemies that this animal is dangerous. Threatened by a larger creature, a skunk may stamp its feet and raise its tail in warning. If that does not work, it turns its back and sprays its enemy with a smelly fluid stored in glands under its tail. Its spray can nearly blind and choke a fox that is up to 13 feet away. Striped skunks live in woods and grasslands in North America.

**Wolverine**    Three feet long and weighing only about 40 pounds, the wolverine is powerful and fearless enough to kill a reindeer. It can gallop, swim, and climb and lives in Arctic lands and northern forests.
***Threatened Species***

**Black-footed ferret**    This small, masked prairie hunter, which preys on prairie dogs, was once thought to be extinct. Its numbers had severely shrunk as American ranchers killed off the prairie dogs. For years no one saw a wild black-footed ferret. Then, in 1981, one was killed by a Wyoming rancher's dog. Soon scientists found more, but disease was wiping them out. People caught any they could find and bred them. By 1990 zoos had more than 120 of the rare carnivores.
***Threatened Species***

**Polecat**    Wild, wooded countryside is home to Europe's equivalent of the black-footed ferret. Polecats seem to glide along almost like snakes as they follow scent trails left by rabbits, rats, and mice. Because they also kill chickens, the French named them *poule chat*, which means "chicken cat." A foul-smelling scent used for marking territory also earned polecats their old English name of *foumart*, or "foul-marten."

**Tayra**    Tayras are slim, restless hunters that weigh about the same as very small dogs. They run fast, swim, climb trees, and plunge down into rodents' burrows. Tree squirrels, chickens, and guinea pigs are also in danger when a tayra is near. Tayras roam the woodlands between Mexico and Argentina.

**Pine marten**    These European martens chase squirrels from branch to branch in forests. Like North American martens, they look like ferrets adapted for climbing. Martens have large, sharp-clawed hands for gripping and a long, bushy tail to help them keep their balance.

# Carnivores, 7

Of all carnivores, cats are probably the most able killers. They have forward-facing eyes; strong, supple bodies; sharp, retractable claws to grasp prey; and strong jaws with sharp teeth to slice through flesh. Most cats wait in ambush or creep up on their prey and then pounce.

There are about three dozen kinds of cats, all shaped much like the domestic house cat. Small cats purr but cannot roar. Big cats roar but cannot purr.

**Bobcat** This cat has a stumpy tail and is like a lynx but prefers more open country and weighs about 25 pounds. Bobcats range from Canada to Mexico.

**Wildcat** Its large size, short legs, and thick, striped fur set this cat apart from its tame descendants. It lives in rocky, wooded regions of Europe and southwestern Asia.

**Fishing cat** Fishing cats come from southern Asia. They are good swimmers and hunt small mammals and waterfowl but catch few, if any, fish. They look like powerfully built tabby cats.

**Ocelot** This lovely, long-legged cat measures about 5 feet long and is strong enough to kill a wild pig. It lives in South America and in the American Southwest but has been heavily hunted for its fur.
***Threatened Species***

**Spanish lynx** This lynx has more spots than the common lynx but might be a member of the same species. Spain now has only a few hundred left, all living in forests.
***Threatened Species***

**Jungle cat** The jungle cat is about the size of a terrier. It kills hares, pheasants, and even peacocks. Its habitats include swampy forests and fields of grain in regions as widespread as Egypt and Thailand.

**Flatheaded cat** This rare species, which lives in southeastern Asia, has unusually short legs and a short tail. One of the smallest cats, it weighs only 4 or 5 pounds. In Borneo the species lives near rivers and catches frogs and fish.

**Sand cat**   The dry semideserts of North Africa and southwestern Asia are home to the sand cat. Sand cats may spend most of the day hiding from the sun in holes in the ground or among rocks. They hunt at night.

**Jaguarundi**   Its small head and ears, short legs, and agile body make the jaguarundi look almost otterlike. Solid gray, brown, or black, the jaguarundi is around 4 feet long and hunts birds and rodents in bushy areas from Texas south to Argentina.

**Margay**   Its beautifully marked coat makes the margay look like a smaller, slimmer version of the ocelot. It, too, has been overhunted for its fur. An agile tree climber, it is found from Mexico to Paraguay. ***Threatened Species***

**Caracal**   The caracal has tufted ears, like a lynx, but a long-legged walk, like a serval. This tall, agile cat can leap almost 7 feet high to grab a bird in flight. Let loose among pigeons feeding on the ground, a caracal can kill 10 of them in the time it would take the birds to fly off. Wild caracals live on the hot African grasslands and in the drier parts of southwestern Asia. Here they will suddenly pop out from the undergrowth and hurl themselves on an unsuspecting mouse, hare, or guinea fowl. Sometimes a young antelope or even a roosting eagle is brought down by the caracal.

**Lynx**   The lynx resembles a large house cat with tufted ears and a stumpy tail. The exact color of its fur varies according to where it lives. Furry feet help it walk on snow without sinking, and it can also climb trees. Because a lynx cannot run fast, it prefers to ambush its prey or to creep up on it and then make a sudden spring. Lynxes kill rabbits and rodents and may also attack deer and sheep. They hunt mostly in the evenings. Most lynxes live in the cold northern forests that stretch across Europe, Asia, and North America.

**Puma**   Also called the panther, mountain lion, or cougar, the puma is as big as a leopard yet in some ways more closely resembles a house cat. Both have a small head for their size, both purr, and neither grasps food with its paws, as lions and tigers do. A large male puma may weigh 200 pounds, with an appetite to match. It can easily kill a deer. What it cannot eat right away it will hide for later. Pumas roam from the cool forests of Alaska through the sweltering jungles of South America to the cold southern end of Chile.

**Serval**   This long-legged cat is as heavy as a medium-sized dog but is more delicately built, with large ears on a small head and a lively, graceful way of walking. It lives in open, bushy parts of Africa, hunting for rodents and pouncing on them when they leave their holes. A serval will leap to knock down a bird that is just taking off, or climb high to seize a tree hyrax.

**Pallas's cat**   Two hundred years ago the German explorer Peter Pallas found a small, stocky, short-legged cat. Its homelands are Central Asia's cold deserts, steppes, and mountains. By day it rests in its rocky den; at night it hunts hares, rabbits, pikas, and rodents. A very thick coat guards this cat from intense cold and makes it seem larger than it is.

**Leopard cat**   Think of a house cat spotted like a leopard and you know what a leopard cat looks like. It climbs and swims extremely well. People in a fishing boat once caught one swimming in the Bay of Bengal. The species may have reached some islands in southeastern Asia that way. This is the commonest wildcat of that area, though leopard cats are also found from India to China. They kill animals as big as deer.

**Black-footed cat**   Africa's smallest wildcat gets its name from the black fur on the bottom of its feet. It also bears the nickname of anthill tiger because of its ferocious snarl and because it likes to spend the day asleep in the hollow, anthill-like nests of termites. Black-footed cats come out to hunt at night, and they kill mice with a quick bite to the neck. If mice are hard to find, the cats will eat insects or spiders.

# Carnivores, 8

It is not only their size that distinguishes big cats from small cats: most of the big cats roar instead of purr. The ability to roar comes from a special kind of bone in the throat. Oddly enough, snow leopards do not roar, although they have the same bone.

Lions, tigers, leopards, and jaguars can all kill prey bigger than themselves, usually by knocking down a victim and biting its neck. Cows or very big antelopes with horns may be seized by the throat and suffocated.

**Cheetah** Long, strong legs make cheetahs the fastest of all land animals. A cheetah will walk toward a small antelope grazing on open grassland and then break into a trot. As the antelope turns and dashes off, the cheetah will chase it at up to 60 miles an hour. If it catches up, the cat will knock the antelope over with one paw and kill it with a bite to the neck. Cheetahs roam the African savannas, and a few still survive on the plains of southwestern Asia.
*Threatened Species*

**Snow leopard** Every summer, snow leopards climb high up the rocky, snowy slopes of the Himalayas and other Asian mountain ranges. Thick fur keeps these big cats warm in the thin, chilly air. Their drab coat blends with the rocks and hides them from the wild sheep and goats they hunt. Snow leopards often stalk their prey, creeping up and then springing. They can jump several yards to cross a broad chasm. A Russian scientist once claimed that he saw a snow leopard leap a 50-foot gap. In autumn, snow leopards grow an extra-long, thick coat and follow their prey down to the forests in the foothills of the mountains.
*Threatened Species*

**Lion** The "king of beasts" is the world's second biggest cat. It lives mostly in Africa, where it is the largest, most powerful carnivore. With their large manes, male lions are splendid-looking animals, weighing up to 500 pounds and measuring 8 feet long. The lionesses are smaller and do not have a mane. Up to 3 lions and 15 lionesses and their cubs form a "pride" to keep other lions out of the group's hunting territory. These big cats often hunt as a team. One lioness may drive an antelope or a zebra toward other lionesses crouched in tall grass. After the kill they all share the meat.

**Leopard** This powerful cat weighs no more than 125 pounds but is strong enough to haul a dead antelope up a tree, out of the reach of hungry lions or hyenas. Leopards are great climbers and spend a lot of time lying on a branch resting or looking for their next meal — perhaps a wild pig, a monkey, or an antelope. A few leopards become man-eaters. In the early 1900s one leopard killed 400 villagers before a hunter shot it. Leopards live in southern Asia and Africa but are becoming scarcer as the forests continue to shrink.

**Clouded leopard** Among the big cats, the clouded leopard is by far the smallest. Many individuals reach only half a common leopard's length and less than half its weight. Clouded leopards are well camouflaged by dark blotches of fur with lighter-colored "clouded" centers, so they are hard to spot in the jungles from India through southeastern Asia. Clouded leopards are so quiet that you could walk under one crouched on a leafy branch without even noticing it was there. These leopards pounce on prey as big as young buffalo but usually leave people alone.
*Threatened Species*

**Jaguar** The jaguar looks like a big leopard. It is the largest cat of the Americas, weighing up to 200 pounds. Jaguars once lived in the United States, but today few survive outside the tropics in South and Central America. They are good climbers and swimmers, hunting capybaras and other water prey. A jaguar will lie alongside a river and scoop up fish with a paw, dig up turtle eggs to eat, or roll turtles onto their backs to pull off their shells.
*Threatened Species*

Its striped coat perfectly camouflages an Indian tiger lying in long grass or padding across a forest floor lit by the dappled sunlight that shines down through the trees. Tigers prowl in search of monkeys, wild boars, and deer. A few eat people. When a tiger stalks its prey, it crouches and then creeps forward until it is near enough to spring. Knocking down its prey, the hunter snaps its neck if the animal is small. It grabs bigger prey by the throat. After killing, the tiger eats until it is full, then hides the rest. The next night it will come back to finish off the rotting remains.

Indian tigers live in India and Bangladesh. Other tigers are found in places from Siberia to southeastern Asia.

**Sumatran tiger**   Like other warm-weather tigers, this one is fairly small, with a short, colorful coat. Only a few hundred survive in the tangled forests on the island of Sumatra. Hunting, poisoning, and the clearing of the land have reduced their numbers. Farmers have only now begun to realize that the tigers were helping them by killing the wild pigs that attacked their crops.
*Threatened Species*

**Caspian tiger**   This medium-sized tiger had long, dark, thick fur and lots of brown stripes all close together. Long ago it lived in Asia from Turkey to Mongolia. But people hunted this tiger, and its homeland shrank to the wild mountain forests in Iran and Russia near the Caspian Sea. Only 15 were believed left by 1970. Since then even those have died.

**Siberian tiger**   We think of tigers as living in hot climates, but the Siberian tiger lives in northeastern Asia, where winters are bitterly cold. This rare tiger grows a long, shaggy coat for protection, and its great size helps its body to store heat. Weighing over 700 pounds, Siberian tigers are the largest of all the cats.
*Threatened Species*

Siberia

Caspian Sea

China

India

Sumatra

Bali

Java

**White Indian tiger**   Now and then a normal Indian tiger gives birth to a cub with almost white rather than reddish fur. Although it has dark brown stripes, its eyes may be icy blue and its nose and paw pads pink. Such rare white tigers were greatly prized as trophies in the days of tiger hunts. In 1951 a white male was caught alive and bred from. His white descendants now live in zoos in India and elsewhere.

**Indian tiger**   Black stripes on a bright reddish-tan coat make this a very striking tiger. Some 40,000 Indian tigers prowled the forests of India in 1900, but hunting and forest destruction killed off all but 1,800 by 1972. At that time, India passed laws to protect them. Since then they have multiplied, but it is too soon to tell if the species has been saved.
*Threatened Species*

**How tigers spread**
Zoologists think the first tigers lived in northeastern Asia perhaps a million years ago. Some spread west to the Caspian Sea area, some south to India and Indonesia. The rising waters stranded many on the islands of Bali, Java, and Sumatra. Isolated groups became different sub-species, with the smallest and darkest in the south, the largest and palest in the north.

# Carnivores, 9

These carnivores hunt and swim in oceans, rivers, seas, or lakes. Steering with limbs modified into flippers, they zoom and dive gracefully beneath the waves. On land it is different. Earless seals thump along awkwardly. Fur seals, sea lions, and walruses can swing their hind flippers forward, enabling them to travel faster. Fur seals and sea lions also have fleshy outer ears that you can see.

**Californian sea lion** At breeding time up to 10,000 of these barking seals will crowd a single island beach off California. Each bull (male) tries to defend a piece of ground against rivals. Trained Californian sea lions can do difficult balancing acts.

**Bearded seal** Long white whiskers that look like a mustache may help this seal find shellfish on the seabed. Crunching up the shells wears down the seal's teeth. This large northern seal measures 10 feet long and weighs up to 800 pounds. It lives along the coasts of the Arctic Ocean.

**Elephant seal** With bulging trunklike noses, these are the biggest of all seals. The males weigh more than 3 tons and measure 18 feet. One species breeds around Antarctica, another off California and Mexico.

**Galápagos sea lion** This sea lion has a smaller head than the Californian sea lion but is very closely related otherwise. Tens of thousands of these mammals thrive on the rocky Galápagos Islands off Ecuador.

**Weddell seal** This champion diver can plunge 2,000 feet to fish for an hour before coming up to breathe through a hole in the ice. Weddell seals swim in the icy seas around Antarctica, and their pups are born on ice floes in the cold Antarctic spring.

**Mediterranean monk seal** A few monk seals survive off rocky Mediterranean coasts, but tourists have taken over most of their breeding beaches. The similar Hawaiian monk seal is also in trouble.
***Threatened Species***

**Walrus** Walruses are big, heavy animals found in the cold Arctic Ocean. They eat shellfish by sucking out the meat. To haul themselves from the sea, they hook their great ivory tusks into floating slabs of ice. They are usually brown but turn reddish when sunbathing in warm weather.

**Hooded seal** An excited male hooded seal blows up loose skin on top of his head until it bulges like a hood. Hooded seals can also inflate a nostril, making it look like a red balloon. These large Arctic seals can grow to 12 feet long and weigh 1,000 pounds.

**Baikal seal** About 300,000 years ago some Arctic Ocean seals swam upriver in Siberia to Lake Baikal, the deepest lake on Earth. Their descendants still live there, far from any sea. Baikal seals are about 5 feet long and weigh about 250 pounds. Pups are born in March in snow-covered caves on the frozen surface of the lake.

**Northern fur seal** From a hilly island in the chilly Bering Sea you can glimpse more large mammals than from any other place on Earth. There, 100,000 northern fur seals come ashore to breed. Big bulls (males), which may weigh up to 700 pounds, rush about, keeping the much smaller cows (females) in check and bellowing at rival males. Yelping black pups romp around in nursery groups. Scenes like this occur on a number of Bering Sea islands. Each spring, up to 1.5 million fur seals visit the area.

**Gray seal** Gray or Atlantic seals may be any color, from silver to almost black. Males can grow to 10 feet long and weigh more than 600 pounds, the size of a pony. The mournful cries of females gave rise to legends of seal-women who lured sailors to their death. Gray seals live off North Atlantic coastlines.

**Harbor seal** This is the most common seal living in the cooler waters of the northern hemisphere. It also spends more time onshore than does any other seal. Large herds rest and sleep together, but individual seals hunt alone. Males measure about 5 feet long and may weigh more than 150 pounds. Females are smaller. Both males and females are gray with black spots. Newborn pups are white.

**Harp seal** This Arctic seal grows to about 6 feet long and is quite heavy (up to 400 pounds), owing to a thick layer of insulating body fat. In early spring, females give birth to pups on rough sea ice. Hunters used to club many thousands of these pups to death, to sell their soft white fur for making the trim on sealskin coats. The cruelty horrified many people, and they stopped buying sealskin coats. Much of the killing has now stopped.

**Leopard seal** These half-ton seals are spotted, like a leopard, and are very aggressive. Although they eat large amounts of fish and shrimplike krill, they will also eat penguins and the young of other seals. A leopard seal that once shot up through a hole in the ice chased a man across the frozen sea. These seals live in the ocean around Antarctica.

**Crabeater seal** Crabeater seals swim along with their mouths wide open, allowing them to fill with krill and water. Then they squirt the water out between their teeth, which form a kind of sieve. Crabeaters live around Antarctica and are quite plentiful.

# Whales, 1

Although seals move awkwardly on land, they can get around. Whales, however, have become completely adapted to life in the sea. They are born in water and can never leave it. Yet whales are mammals, and so, unlike fish, they must come to the surface to breathe.

Whales fall into two basic groups: baleen and toothed. On these two pages are pictures of 9 of the 10 kinds of baleen whales. One of them is the largest animal that has ever lived. Baleen whales do not have teeth. Instead, horny baleen plates hang down from the upper jaws like giant fringed combs. The plates act as sieves, trapping millions of tiny shrimplike creatures while the whales swim near the surface of the sea with their huge mouths wide open.

**Blue whale**  The largest animal that has ever lived, the blue whale can grow to 100 feet long and weigh 180 tons. Its tongue alone weighs as much as an elephant, and babies are as long as a bus. Adults eat over 4 tons of shrimplike krill a day. This whale's whistle is louder than a passing jet.
***Threatened Species***

**Gray whale**  This Pacific whale migrates over 14,000 miles each year —farther than any other mammal. It swims south from its Arctic feeding grounds to breed off Mexico, then swims back north to feed again. Gray whales can grow to 45 feet long and weigh up to 35 tons.

**Finback whale**  This whale is also called the common rorqual. *Rorqual* is a Norwegian word for the grooves that allow the whale's throat to stretch when it feeds. At up to 80 feet long and weighing 100 tons, the finback whale may be the second largest animal in the world. It is certainly the fastest great whale, swimming at almost 25 miles per hour.
***Threatened Species***

**Minke whale**  Minkes are small, chunky rorquals with narrow, pointed heads. They can reach 25 feet in length and weigh 9 tons. Besides eating krill, they will open their mouths wide and swim rapidly up through a shoal of small fish. Minkes live in most oceans.

**Humpback whale**    Huge flippers — up to 12 feet long — and a deep, humped back that shows as it dives distinguish this whale. Humpbacks can grow to over 50 feet long and weigh 50 tons, but they can leap right out of the water. Antarctic and Arctic groups breed in the tropics.
***Threatened Species***

**Bryde's whale**    Bryde's (pronounced Brewders) whale gets its name from a Norwegian who set up a factory for whale products in South Africa. This rorqual (see Finback whale, page 54), which regularly visits the tropics, eats mainly fish. The species looks like a sei whale but is a little smaller and has three ridges on its head. Bryde's whale swims near ships to inspect them.
***Threatened Species***

**Bowhead whale**    Bowheads get their name from their huge, bow-shaped skull, which accounts for about a third of their total length. The immense animals grow up to 60 feet long and weigh up to 80 tons. They live in and near the Arctic Ocean.
***Threatened Species***

**Great right whale**    Clumps of barnacles on its head make this whale easy to identify. Great right whales can grow up to 50 feet long and weigh nearly 80 tons. The northern and southern oceans have quite different populations.
***Threatened Species***

**Sei whale**    With its flat, stream-lined head, the sei whale is a typical rorqual. It grows up to 60 feet long, weighs 30 tons, and eats a ton a day of small, shrimplike krill, squid, and fish. Couples may mate for life. Sei whales swim in almost all oceans.

# Whales, 2

Most whales — more than 60 kinds — have teeth. Some have as many as 200, which they use for seizing fish or squid. Toothed whales include sperm, beaked, white, killer, and pilot whales, plus dolphins, river dolphins, and porpoises. The biggest toothed whale can weigh as much as six elephants, but the smallest is no bigger than a large dog. To track down prey, they all make clicking sounds that bounce off objects and return to them as echoes. Then they home in on the object's location to seize their food.

**Orca or killer whale**   The largest big-game hunter of the seas can grow 30 feet long and weigh 7 tons. With its great toothy jaws, it will tackle sharks, seals, and even other whales. The stomach of one that was caught was said to contain 14 seals and 13 porpoises. Orcas roam the oceans in packs called "pods."

**False killer whale**   This slim whale is about 15 feet long and swims in groups, making piercing whistles. Mothers may hold in their mouths fish they have caught, for their young to eat later.

**Sperm whale**   This is the largest toothed whale. Males average 50 feet in length and 40 tons in weight. This whale's huge head contains large amounts of spermaceti wax. As this wax melts and freezes, it may help the creature to sink and rise in the water. Sperm whales can dive at least 3,000 feet to ambush giant squid and some sharks, holding their breath for about 45 minutes. A sperm whale may eat a ton of squid daily.

**Pilot whale**   This slim black whale grows up to 20 feet long. Pilot whales make buzzing, chirping, snoring, squeaking, and whistling sounds, among others. Because they follow a leader, a whole group can be stranded if its leader swims ashore. They inhabit all cool oceans.

**Commerson's or piebald dolphin**   The cold, shallow inshore waters off southern South America are home to this 4-foot-long, tubby whale. Scientists suspect that the species is becoming rare.

**Beluga**   Also known as the white whale, the beluga resembles a small narwhal without a tusk. Belugas swim in Arctic rivers and seas, sometimes pushing aside ice floes to get air. They are becoming scarce.

**Narwhal**   The male grows about as long as a false killer whale and has a long tusk. Rival males probably threaten one another with their tusk, although divers have also seen them using it to scrape the seabed, as if searching for food. Narwhals live in cold, Arctic waters but are becoming scarce.

**Black-chin dolphin**    Not much is known about this small whale, which is found only in cold waters off the southern tip of South America. It grows to about 6 feet long and usually swims in groups of 3 or 4, though up to 50 have been seen together. Black-chin dolphins feed at least partly on octopuses and other creatures that live on the ocean floor.

**Atlantic humpbacked dolphin** The long hump on this dolphin's back looks like a backpack with a tiny fin added. When the dolphin rises to the surface to breathe, its long, narrow beak appears first, followed by its bulging head and humped back. The species lives only off the coast of West Africa.

**Spectacled porpoise** A wide ring around each eye gives this animal its name. Like other true porpoises, this is a small whale without a beak. What we know about it comes mostly from remains washed ashore on South American coasts.

**Black porpoise**    This small, tubby porpoise, also known as Burmeister's porpoise, is not much larger than the Benguela dolphin and is another little-known whale. From specimens caught in fishing nets, it seems that black porpoises live in the chilly waters on both sides of southern South America.

**Black dolphin**    About the same size as the Benguela dolphin, this species is found only in the cold coastal waters of Chile. It is also called the Chilean dolphin. Fishing crews use its flesh as crab bait. The black dolphin may be another rare whale that is threatened.

**Indo-Pacific humpbacked dolphin**    Like its slightly larger Atlantic Ocean relative, this dolphin looks as if it is wearing a backpack. The species feeds near mangrove swamps. It leaps and twists in the air and even performs back somersaults.

**Short-snout dolphin** Although a bit longer than the other dolphins described, this dolphin weighs less — about 200 pounds. Zoologists once considered short-snout dolphins to be one of the world's rarest whales. They now know that these dolphins are common in all warm oceans. One whale watcher even spotted a "school" with as many as 500 traveling together.

**Benguela dolphin**    One of the tiniest whales, the Benguela dolphin is less than 4 feet long. It lives in cold waters off southwestern Africa, but very few have been seen. Some people think this already rare whale is becoming even more rare.

**Bottlenose dolphin**    Bottlenose dolphins are often seen performing at marine shows. These strong, streamlined whales usually grow to about 10 feet in length and weigh 400 pounds. They sometimes help each other, with two raising an injured companion to the surface so it can breathe. A school (group) may even work together catching fish. While some eat, others stop the fish from escaping.

**Harbor porpoise**    The cool, shallow waters of the North Atlantic and North Pacific oceans are home to this tubby, toothed whale. Harbor porpoises grow only about 5 feet long and weigh less than 100 pounds. Playful groups hunt mackerel, herring, or other fish. Harbor porpoises are less common than they used to be.

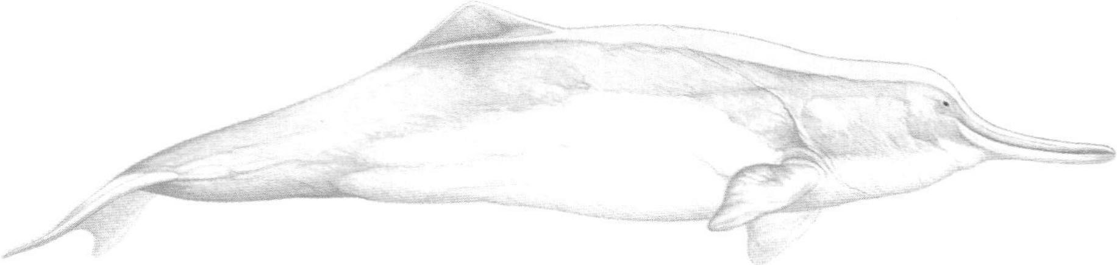

**Baiji**    *Baiji* is Chinese for "the gray-white dolphin," which is also called the Chinese river dolphin because of the muddy Yangtze River, which is its home. Baijis are almost blind. They hunt by using sound echoes, catching fish and crustaceans in their toothy beaks.
***Threatened Species***

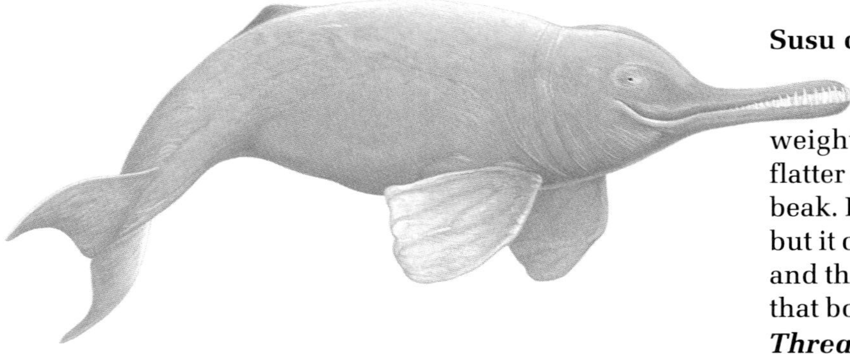

**Susu or Indus river dolphin**    This river dolphin is about the size and weight of a harbor porpoise but has a flatter forehead and a long, toothy beak. Its tiny eyes can scarcely see, but it catches fish by making sounds and then tracking down the echoes that bounce back. It lives in India.
***Threatened Species***

**Finless porpoise**    As its name suggests, the finless porpoise has no fin, just a low ridge on its back. This tiny whale measures about 5 feet long and weighs 100 pounds. It feeds on shrimp and squid in muddy river mouths off the coasts of China and India.

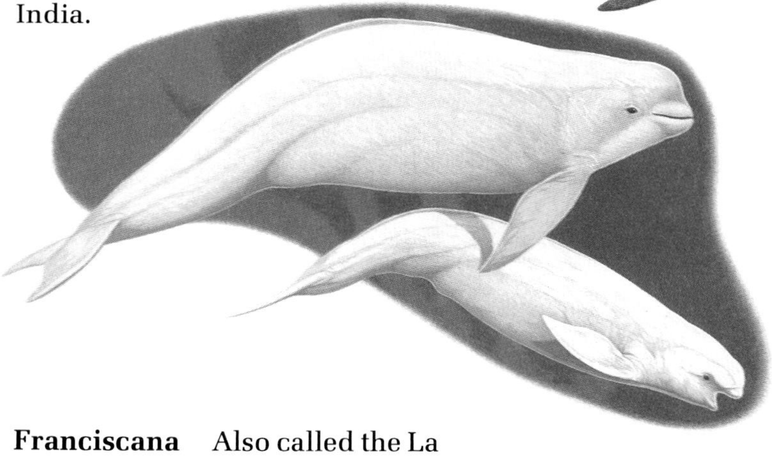

**Amazon river dolphin, or bouto**    This dolphin makes sneezing snorts, which is one meaning of the Portuguese word *bouto.* Up to 8 feet long but slim-bodied, this dolphin lives far up the Amazon River — up to more than 2,500 miles from the sea. When the river overflows its banks, the Amazon river dolphin will search for fish in the flooded forest.

***Threatened Species***

**Franciscana**    Also called the La Plata river dolphin, this little whale lives offshore and in the mouths of big rivers along the eastern coast of South America. Its toothy beak is long and narrow, and a fin juts up from its back. The franciscana is about the same size and weight as a harbor porpoise. It may be disappearing.

58

# Anteaters, sloths, and armadillos

Armadillos, sloths, and true anteaters are American mammals. Those that eat ants and termites flick out a long, sticky tongue to catch their tiny prey. Because these mammals have little need for teeth that bite or chew, their teeth have shrunk or vanished. Scientists call them *edentates*, or "toothless" mammals.

Pangolins from Africa and southeastern Asia are toothless, too. But they are not related to the American anteaters they resemble.

**Pygmy anteater**   This tiny forest anteater from South and Central America has a head and body about as long as a person's hand. Silky fur earns it the nickname of silky anteater. The animal climbs trees, gripping with its tail as it licks up ants. If an owl or eagle attacks, it lashes out with its big, hooklike claws.

**Tamandua**   This climbing anteater has a head and body up to 3 feet long. One kind lives only in South America, another in both South and Central America. They all sleep in hollow trees by day and hunt by night. The tail acts as an extra hand. Bare skin on the tail's underside grips branches while the tamandua's hooked claws rip open ant or termite nests.

**Tree pangolin**   Overlapping scales make pangolins look like living pine cones. Rolled up, they are almost impossible — even for leopards — to attack. Although tree pangolins are not closely related to tamanduas, they, too, climb trees to eat ants and have a tail that grips, a long and sticky tongue, and toothless jaws.

**Giant anteater**   This is the largest anteater. Including its bushy tail, it may be 8 feet long. The tail helps the anteater shade its body from the sun as it roams hot, grassy parts of South America. It rips open termite nests with claws so long it has to walk on its knuckles. To catch termites, it flicks out a sticky, yard-long tongue.

**Three-toed sloth**   Three hooklike claws on its long arms help a three-toed sloth hang upside down for hours or creep along a branch to feed on leaves. It seldom comes down from the trees; when it does, it must come down backwards. Three species live in South America. One is the slowest of all land mammals. Another is becoming scarce as the forests where it lives in southeastern Brazil are cut down.
***Threatened Species***

**Two-toed sloth**   Both species of this sloth have only two front claws. Two-toed sloths move a little faster than their three-toed relatives and can even climb down trees head-first. They live in the rainforests of South America. As with all sloths, their hair grows upward, so the rain just runs off it as they hang upside down.

**Giant armadillo**   This is easily the biggest armadillo, about 5 feet long, including the tail. Propped up by its tail and back legs, it digs deep into termite mounds with the long claws on its front feet. In addition to termites, it eats ants, worms, and snakes. This heavy South American mammal has more than twice as many teeth as most mammals, but they are small and fall out as the animal ages.
***Threatened Species***

**Three-banded armadillo**   Two, three, or four bands of armor-like skin are found around the middle of this armadillo, between its rounded hips and shoulders. This is the only armadillo able to roll itself into a tight ball to protect every part of its body. Its defense is so good that the armadillo does not need to burrow. It lives in Brazil, Paraguay, and Bolivia.

**Hairy armadillo**   Long hairs between its armored bands explain this armadillo's name. If attacked, hairy armadillos wedge themselves in deep burrows. They live on the grasslands of Argentina and nearby countries.

**Six-banded armadillo**   Around its middle this armadillo has six armored bands, with long tufts of hair between them. The creature is rather flat from top to bottom and so digs a low, wide tunnel. It is native to lands east of the Andes in South America.

**Pichi**   Scuttling about like little mechanical toys, pichis hunt for beetles and birds' eggs. Some of them visit seashores to feed on dead crabs. Thick white hair and a heavy layer of body fat help keep them warm in chilly Patagonia, but winters there grow so cold that the creatures probably hibernate.

**Naked-tailed armadillo**   Four kinds of South American armadillo go by this name. Their unusually soft tails are covered by thin, delicate scales. All kinds have five big claws on their front feet. The curved middle claw is the largest.

**Nine-banded armadillo**   This armadillo thrives from Argentina to Mexico. It reached and rapidly spread across parts of the United States about 100 years ago. Nine-banded armadillos have succeeded because they eat almost any small animal, can breed at any time of year, and almost always produce four identical babies at a time. Nine bands of armorlike, bony plates encircle this armadillo, and it is the only kind to grow two sets of teeth. Like most armadillos, it is a great digger and can disappear into hard ground in two minutes.

**Greater fairy or Burmeister's armadillo**   This armadillo behaves and looks very much like the lesser fairy armadillo, its relative. However, this armadillo's entire back shield, not just a strip down the middle, is attached to skin. It burrows in the grasslands of northern Argentina and is rapidly disappearing.

**Lesser fairy armadillo**   This pink-and-white mammal is the tiniest armadillo. It measures only about 5 inches long. Horny bands guard its back but not its sides. It protects its burrow with a shield of armor that covers its rear. Armor is not vital to this animal, who spends most of its time underground. Its tiny eyes, soft fur, and strong digger's front feet make it look like a mole. As farmers have plowed up Argentina's grass-lands, this armadillo has become scarce.

# Elephants and related species

Elephants, sea cows, hyraxes, and aardvarks have very different shapes, yet scientists suspect that they are all related to one another.

**Dugong**   This sea mammal has flipper-shaped "arms," a split tail, and two nipples on the chest. It is about 9 feet long and weighs about 750 pounds. Tales of mermaids may have begun when sailors saw dugongs swim up to breathe. Dugongs graze on underwater weeds off the warm shores of the Indian Ocean and the southwestern Pacific. Their back teeth are worn down by chewing but continue to grow throughout their lives.
***Threatened Species***

**Tree hyrax**   Hyraxes may look like small rabbits, but horses or perhaps even elephants appear to be their nearest relatives. Tree hyraxes live in the wooded parts of Africa, where they munch on leaves high above the ground. Springy, padded feet with clawlike nails help them run up even smooth tree trunks, and special sticky secretions on their feet give them an even better grip. These noisy little mammals usually live in pairs.

**Manatee**   Manatees, also called sea cows, look like dugongs, but their flattened tails are paddle-shaped. They grow new teeth to replace some of the old ones that wear out. Manatees swim up rivers and graze on freshwater plants that are too tough for a dugong. The West Indian and West African species are the largest sea cows, up to 12 feet long and weighing about 1,000 pounds. A mother sea cow chirps and squeals to her calf and looks after it for months.
***Threatened Species***

**African elephant**   The world's largest land mammal stands 10 feet tall and weighs up to 6 tons. Its ears are bigger than an Indian elephant's, its trunk has two fingerlike tips, and its back sags in the middle. Both males and females have tusks for defense. African and Indian elephants roam in herds of females and young that are led by an old female. Females help one another mind the young. Males often live alone. In one day a big bull can eat 500 pounds of leaves and drink 50 gallons of water.
***Threatened Species***

**Indian elephant**   The world's second largest land mammal has smaller ears than an African elephant and a humped or level back. It has only one fingerlike tip on its trunk, which is sensitive and flexible enough to pick up a coin. Many of the females lack tusks. Indian elephants live in southern and southeastern Asia.
***Threatened Species***

**Aardvark**   This name is South African for "earth pig." An aardvark is indeed piglike and a burrower. It lives in Africa and tears open termite nests with its claws, catching the insects with its sticky tongue.

**Rock hyrax**   This tree hyrax look-alike scampers over rocks. Dozens of rock hyraxes feed together while a few keep watch and bark a warning if an eagle appears. Five species live in Africa. One species is also found in southwestern Asia.

# Even-toed hoofed mammals, 1

Wild pigs and their relatives, the peccaries, are quick, agile creatures that are very different from domesticated pigs. Pigs are Old World animals, but peccaries live only in the Americas. Both groups have a big head, a long snout for rooting about, tusklike canine teeth, and short legs with four hoofed toes on each foot.

Along with cattle, deer, and some other related species, pigs and peccaries form the artiodactyls, which are mammals with an even number of hoofed toes. Most artiodactyls are herbivores, but pigs and peccaries go through woods and grasslands eating almost anything, from roots and insects to worms and mice.

**Giant forest hog** Reaching about 6 feet long and weighing up to 500 pounds, the world's largest wild pig well deserves its name. The adult's dark face and hair look almost like a gorilla's, but its eyes are set much deeper into the face. These shy animals live in the dense African rainforests. They remained unknown until 1904.

**Warthog** Big, wartlike bumps on its face make this a very ugly animal to most people. Large, curved tusks are its main defense. A warthog chased by lions will try to back into a hole and face its enemies. Warthog families share a stretch of African grassland that has water to drink, mud to wallow in, and perhaps aardvark burrows where they can rest in safety.

**Wild boar** With its long snout, lean body, and muscular legs, the wild boar of Asia, Europe, and North Africa doesn't look much like its descendant, the domesticated pig. Whole families of wild boars sniff the forest floor together looking for acorns and tasty roots. Wild boars are brave fighters and will sometimes charge a human hunter, tearing deep gashes in the flesh with their tusks.

**Pygmy hog** This is the smallest wild pig. It is no bigger than a small dog. Despite its tiny size, the pygmy hog is as brave as the wild boar. If disturbed, it will attack animals much bigger than itself. Large groups of pygmy hogs, called "sounders," roam the hillsides in the forests of Nepal and northern India.
***Threatened Species***

**Collared peccary** Roots, seeds, and fruits are favorite foods of this New World relative of the pig. Herds of as many as 50 collared peccaries rummage through woods and forests from the United States to Argentina. If a jaguar appears, one peccary may stay behind to face it, giving the rest time to escape.

**Babirusa** Male babirusas have two pairs of large tusks, with one pair sprouting from the skin above the snout. These almost hairless Indonesian pigs can swim and sometimes even swim in the ocean.
***Threatened Species***

**Red river hog** This hog can be quite colorful, with a reddish coat, wiry white whiskers, and black markings on its head. Mature males lead family groups of up to 10 as they forage through wooded areas and fields in Africa south of the Sahara Desert. Red river hogs also live on the island of Madagascar. Because they trample and root up crops, these pigs are not liked by African farmers.

# Even-toed hoofed mammals, 2

The name *hippopotamus* means "river horse," although hippopotamuses don't look very much like horses (except perhaps when they are mostly submerged in water). Their nearest relatives are pigs. On land, hippopotamuses waddle along awkwardly on stumpy legs that seem too small to hold up their immense, barrel-shaped bodies. In lakes and rivers, where they are buoyed up by the water, they move more gracefully.

**Hippopotamus**
After the elephants and two species of rhinoceros, this is the heaviest land animal.
A big adult hippopotamus may weigh more than 2 tons and grow to 15 feet long, not counting its stumpy tail. It stands about 5 feet tall at the shoulders. The hippopotamus has ears, eyes, and nostrils on top of its large head so it can hear, see, and breathe with just the top of its head above water. Hippopotamuses must spend the day almost totally submerged to escape the hot African sunshine. Otherwise , they would lose too much body water through their thin outer skin and die. At night, hippopotamuses go ashore in groups. They plunge through the tall savanna grasses to fields of short grass, where they graze. Hippopotamuses have few enemies, but during fights males may kill each other with their long, sharp canine teeth.

**Pygmy hippopotamus**
This species is only about half as long and weighs only a tenth as much as a hippopotamus. With a relatively small head and long neck, a full-grown pygmy hippo looks a lot like a young hippopotamus. Its eyes are less bulging, however, and they are located on the sides of the head rather than on top. Its feet are different, too. The pygmy's toes are broader and less webbed and have sharper nails. This smaller hippopotamus also eats more kinds of food and spends a lot of time on land. A frightened pygmy hippopotamus may hurry into the undergrowth instead of plunging into water. The species lives in swamps and rivers in the dense West African forests.
***Threatened Species***

# Even-toed hoofed mammals, 3

In the camel family, only the Asian species have one or two humps on their backs. Four species from South America have no humps. All six known species have a long, curved neck and long legs and rest their weight on soft pads behind their hooves. Rather like deer and cattle, camels chew and swallow food twice before it is digested in a stomach that has several compartments.

**Llama**   Llamas are the largest members of the camel family in South America. Andean Indians use these sure-footed animals to carry loads up narrow mountain trails.

**Alpaca**   Like llamas, alpacas are probably domesticated descendants of the guanaco (see below). The people who live in the mountains of Bolivia and Peru raise them for their long, silky hair, which can be woven into soft, warm cloth.

**Vicuña**   This is the smallest member of the camel family. It has the finest fleece grown by any wool-producing mammal. Its coat helps keep it warm on the high, windswept pastures of the Andes Mountains.
*Threatened Species*

**Guanaco**   Slim, long-limbed, and speedy, guanacos roam the open lands of southern South America. Many are shot for eating the grasses that ranchers try to reserve for their sheep.

**Bactrian camel**   Fat stored in its two humps nourishes this camel as it crosses deserts. Long, shaggy hair keeps it warm through the winter. Only a few wild Bactrian camels still roam Central Asia.
*Threatened Species*

**Dromedary**   This one-humped camel can lose a quarter of its body weight in sweat before it needs to drink. It lives in the hot deserts of North Africa and southwestern Asia.

# Even-toed hoofed mammals, 4

Deer are graceful browsing animals with long, slim legs. They have a horny pad instead of upper front teeth. Most males sprout new antlers every year, but deer would rather run away than stand and fight another animal, such as a wolf.

The little deerlike chevrotains digest plant food in the three compartments in their stomach, but true deer have four compartments in their stomach. They can swallow a meal of leaves out in the open, then hide in the woods while they chew and digest their food again.

**Reindeer**   Scientists now think that reindeer and caribou are just two names for the same species of deer. Caribou live in North America, while reindeer live in Europe and Asia. Many reindeer herds have been domesticated. On all three continents these deer live in colder climates than any other kind of deer. Their homelands are the northern forests and open tundra around the Arctic Ocean. The species is unusual in another way, too: both sexes have antlers. Each antler's lowest branch juts forward and sprouts additional branches. Herds of caribou and reindeer spend the summer grazing on the open tundra. When the snows come in autumn, the herds move southward. They spend the winter in the forests, pawing away snow on the ground to eat the lichens growing underneath.

**Red deer**   Europe's red deer may belong to the same species as the North American elk, or wapiti. Red deer are also found in Africa and Asia. These deer are quite large and have a rust-colored summer coat. Each autumn the males (stags) clash their antlers together to decide who will rule the females (hinds). Red deer roam in herds, browsing on grass and other vegetation.

**Chinese water deer**   This small deer is shorter than a roe deer (see next entry.) It lives along reedy riverbanks in China and Korea and forages at night on grass and reeds. This is one of a few species of deer that lack antlers. Rival males fight anyway, using their canine teeth that jut out and form tusks.

 **Roe deer**   The roe deer is the smallest deer that is native to Europe. It also lives across Asia, to China and Korea. This is the only deer with no visible tail, and its short antlers sprout only three or fewer branches (tines). In the mating season, males rub their antlers on trees to tear the bark. This marks the edges of their territory.

**Moose**   The North American moose and the European elk are members of the same species. They are the largest deer on Earth. A big Alaskan moose may stand more than 6 feet tall at the shoulders and weigh half a ton. The animals roam northern forests and will wade out into swamps to browse on aquatic plants. In the autumn rival males fight each other with their broad antlers which are shaped like giant hands.

**Chinese muntjac deer**   Even smaller than the Chinese water deer, this shy creature lives alone in the dense woodlands of southeastern China. It is seldom seen but can be heard when the males make short barking cries at mating time. This small deer's antlers sprout from high bony knobs called "pedicels." Males and females both have small tusks, but the males fight with theirs.

**Lesser mouse deer**   No bigger than a rabbit, southeastern Asia's lesser mouse deer is the smallest of all deerlike mammals. This shy creature with a mouselike head is a chevrotain, an animal that resembles a pig in some ways and a deer in other ways. It makes small tunnels in the undergrowth as it forages at night for leaves and fallen fruits. The male has tusks but no antlers.

**Water chevrotain**   The water chevrotain from West and Central Africa owes its name to its habit of jumping in a river and swimming away or even diving under the water when disturbed. It is a forest animal, nearly twice as long as a lesser mouse deer and as heavy as a small dog. White stripes and spots mark its reddish brown body.

# Even-toed hoofed mammals, 5

An enormously long neck and long legs make the giraffe the tallest animal alive. Amazingly, this mammal has only seven neck bones — no more than a human being or any other mammal. Of course, its neck bones are much longer.

Being built like a crane on stilts means that a giraffe can feed on tree leaves that are out of reach of the tallest antelopes. It strips them off with its comblike teeth and pulls them into its mouth with a tongue that is longer than a person's forearm.

Giraffes hurry along with a peculiar gait, swinging both legs forward on one side of the body at almost the same time. They can also gallop even faster than a horse, and a cornered giraffe can kill a lion with a kick from one of its plate-sized front hooves.

Several varieties of giraffe roam Africa's savannas and open forests. The only other living member of the giraffe family is the rather horselike okapi, which can be found in the dense tropical forests of Africa.

**Transvaal giraffe** Some people think that these giraffes are a distinct subspecies. They are named after the region they come from. Transvaal is a province in the northeastern region of South Africa.

**Reticulated giraffe** This handsome animal has narrow white lines between reddish markings. It comes from Somalia and northern Kenya. People used to think it was not a subspecies but a completely separate species.

**Masai giraffe** This giraffe has jagged red marks on a yellowish beige background. Its legs are spotted below the knees. The Masai giraffe lives in parts of Kenya, Uganda, and Tanzania.

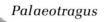

**Baringo giraffe** The baringo's pattern resembles a reticulated giraffe's but is less red. There are no markings below the knees. This giraffe is a subspecies found only in northwestern Kenya and northern Uganda.

**Nubian giraffe** This subspecies comes from the Sudan and Egypt but has been largely killed off.

*Threatened Subspecies*

**Okapi** This mammal is about as heavy as a pony. The okapi is a member of the giraffe family and is a little like a giraffe in that it has long legs and a long tongue and its body slopes down from the shoulders. However, its neck is far shorter than a giraffe's. Okapis are timid forest dwellers that live in northeastern Zaire in Africa.

---

**Prehistoric giraffes**
Today's long-necked giraffe evolved from a prehistoric animal that looked more like an okapi. This creature, called *Palaeotragus*, lived about 15 million years ago.

Other prehistoric giraffes included large, oxlike creatures called sivatheres. *Sivatherium* had big, flat, bony horns. It may have died out only a few thousand years ago.

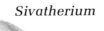

*Palaeotragus*

*Sivatherium*

# Even-toed hoofed mammals, 6

Cattle are among the most numerous grass-eating animals alive today. Their teeth, legs, feet, and stomachs suit these hoofed mammals, with an even number of toes, for a life spent grazing on the open plains. Wild cattle live in Africa and Asia, but domesticated breeds are kept on every continent except Antarctica.

Close cattle relatives include sheep, goats, antelopes, and several smaller groups that are treated separately from cattle in this book. Unlike deer, which shed their antlers every year, these animals keep their horns for life.

**African buffalo**   This powerful animal roams in herds that are led by cows but ruled by mature bulls. It lives on open grasslands and in forests, eating leaves and wallowing in mud. An enraged buffalo will charge a lion. Its strong, horned head makes it very dangerous.

**Yak**   The wild yaks of Tibet may roam higher up than any other mammal. Some may get above 18,000 feet. Their long, silky hair helps keep them warm in the thin, cold mountain air. Wild yaks weigh only about half as much as buffalo and are more agile. They can cross rock slides, pick their way down steep slopes, and swim icy rivers.
***Threatened Species***

**Musk-ox**   Thick fur protects musk-oxen from the fierce cold of Arctic winters, when herds must paw through the snow to get at the mosses and lichens they eat. Their horns help drive off hungry wolves.

**Gaur**   The largest of the wild Asian cattle, a gaur can weigh a ton. From India to southeastern Asia, small herds live in forests. They come out at dusk to graze.
***Threatened Species***

**Zebu**   Brahman is the other name of this type of domesticated cattle. It has a humped back, drooping ears, and a fold of skin called a dewlap hanging under its neck. The breed comes from southern Asia but thrives in many other warm locations.

**Buffalo**   Its humped shoulders and shaggy fur make this big ox easy to recognize. A big male buffalo may weigh a ton and stand 6 feet tall at the shoulders. Millions of buffalo roamed the North American prairies in huge herds until hunters almost wiped them out. About 35,000 currently live in the safety of lands set aside as reserves.

**Highland**   This is a domesticated breed of cattle from the mountains of western Scotland. A shaggy coat protects it from bad weather. It thrives in cold mountain pastures where other native breeds cannot survive and has widespread horns.

# Even-toed hoofed mammals, 7

Flocks of wild sheep and herds of wild goats graze on steep rocky mountain slopes across northern Europe, Asia, and Africa. Few predators can catch these nimble climbers, which can leap from crag to crag. Males are larger than females and are armed with bigger horns, which they use in butting fights.

Goat antelopes are related to sheep and goats and include the chamois and mountain goat. The saiga antelope is a close relative and is shown with the true antelopes.

**Dall sheep**    In autumn the northern Rocky Mountains of the United States echo to the thudding sounds of rival Dall rams banging heads. These sure-footed, snow-white sheep spend the summer high up in grassy pastures. In winter they move down to sheltered valleys.

**Mountain goat**    The mountain goats of northwestern North America can survive winter blizzards that force Dall sheep off the high slopes. They have woolly fur and a coarse outer coat to keep out the cold and wet, and their springy hooves with hard edges grip rocks like climbing boots.

**Spanish ibex**    This wild goat is an agile mountaineer, able to climb an almost sheer rock face. The species lives only in Spain.
*Threatened Species*

**Mouflon**    Domesticated sheep were bred largely from this animal, which leaps and climbs with great energy in the mountains of southwestern Asia and in a few rugged parts of Europe. This is the smallest wild sheep.

**Barbary sheep**    North Africa's only native sheep has a long, soft beard hanging from its throat. Both sexes have large, heavy horns.
*Threatened Species*

**Markhor**    Its spiral horns, long, shaggy beard, and chest hair make the markhor easy to identify. One of the biggest wild goats, it is a good climber and jumper. It lives in the western Himalayas. Hunting and disease have reduced its numbers.
*Threatened Species*

**Chamois**    The Alpine pastures of Europe and steep mountain slopes of southwestern Asia are home to this goat-antelope. Both male and female chamois have horns shaped like hooks. Thanks to its shock-absorbing hooves, a chamois can leap off a rock and land unharmed as much as 25 feet away.

# Even-toed hoofed mammals, 8

Antelopes belong to the cattle family. There are more than 80 kinds of these horned and hoofed mammals. Most move swiftly and are much smaller and slimmer than cattle. Male antelopes are armed with spiral horns. Biggest of all is the giant eland, which weighs as much as an African buffalo. Among the smallest is the blue duiker, as light as a small dog.

Most kinds graze on African savannas and deserts; some live in southern parts of Asia. Where several species feed close together, each kind eats different plants. Their enemies include lions, leopards, and cheetahs.

In the following pages you will meet 15 true antelopes, plus the antelope-like saiga and the pronghorn.

**Giant eland**   This is the largest of all antelopes, a solidly built animal similar to an ox. The biggest males can weigh a ton; the females weigh less. Both sexes grow spiral horns. Small herds munch on leaves and bulbs in the open woodlands of Africa south of the Sahara Desert. Hunters have exterminated some herds.

**Springbok**   This delicate little mammal gets its name from its habit of springing along stiff-legged and landing on all fours when scared or being playful. Huge herds of springboks once roamed southern Africa's dry, open plains.

**Lechwe**   Lechwes are marsh antelopes from southern Africa. Long hooves help support their weight as they walk or leap along on soft mud or springy reeds. If lions chase a herd of lechwes, the antelopes will bound into shallow water, then swim off across a lake or river. ***Threatened Species***

**Impala**   As it runs away from an attacker, this medium-sized African antelope can perform jumps of 40 feet long and several yards high. These antics may confuse the lion or hyena. The male impala has horns resembling a lyre, an ancient harp.

**Greater kudu**   Although he weighs only half as much as a giant eland, a male greater kudu is roughly the same height. Spiral horns over 3 feet long make him even more impressive as he stands with his head held high. Laid back over his shoulders, the horns protect his neck from an attacking lion.

**Oribi**   Oribis are small, graceful African antelopes. They have slim legs, a long, slender neck, and tall, oval-shaped ears. Oribis have many scent glands, which they use to mark out territories. They walk daintily and leap stiff-legged as they run.

**Steenbok**   The steenbok of eastern and southern Africa is even smaller than an oribi and sometimes hides in old aardvark burrows. It roams the grassy plains alone or in pairs, rubbing plant stems with its eyelids, which contain scent glands.

**Nyala**   Males are large, with shaggy, gray-brown coats and slightly curved horns. Females are smaller and redder, with white stripes and no horns. Nyalas live in southeastern Africa, daring to come out of the dense forest only at dawn and dusk.

**Arabian oryx**    Fleeting glimpses of this big white desert antelope might have started legends about the unicorn. These oryxes lived in much of Saudi Arabia until hunters almost wiped them out. The last few were caught and bred, and now their offspring are being returned to the wild.
***Threatened Species***

**Saiga**    Its bulging snout makes the saiga easy to identify. This goat antelope almost died out in the early 1900s. The government of the former Soviet Union protected it, and now millions again roam the grassy plains of Central Asia.

**Brindled gnu**    Also called the blue wildebeest, this cowlike antelope grazes on the grassy plains of eastern and southeastern Africa. It moves clumsily, as herds of thousands migrate up to 1,000 miles to find fresh grass and drinking water. On these journeys, hundreds drown crossing rivers or are attacked by lions, hyenas, or crocodiles.

**Topi**    Topis are very large, reddish brown African antelopes with a back that slopes down from their shoulders. They usually graze in small groups, but several thousand will wander together to reach new feeding grounds. Topis prefer the grass found in valleys near the edges of woodlands. Rival males try to keep each other out of their territory, which can be as much as 1,000 acres.

**Bontebok**    Hunters once almost killed off this handsome antelope with a white face, white rump, and white lower legs. By the early 1900s the last few lived in cattle country in southern Africa. The farmers fenced them in and encouraged them to breed. As their numbers increased, people began moving some to other ranches. Whole herds have recently been released into the wild.
***Threatened Species***

**Gemsbok**    The powerful gemsbok is an oryx found in several very hot, dry parts of Africa. Its silvery coat helps reflect the heat. Special veins cool the blood flowing to its brain, and its shallow breathing also helps it save water. The gemsbok spends the hottest parts of the day in the shade. Both sexes have long, narrow horns. The oryx attacks wild dogs by moving its head from side to side, and rival males lock horns when fighting.

**Gerenuk**    *Gerenuk* means "giraffe-necked." This tall, graceful African antelope has a long, giraffe-like neck that enables it to eat leaves that are out of reach of its smaller relatives. A feeding gerenuk rears up on its long, slim hind legs to reach the juiciest shoots and leaves. It will even balance on its hind legs as it walks around a tree or a shrub. No other antelopes can do that.

**Sable antelope**    This large, horselike antelope has a stiff mane of hair on its back. Males are usually black, but females can be reddish and thus easily mistaken for another species. Both sexes grow long, curved horns. With these dangerous weapons, the sable antelope is quite capable of driving off a lion or a pack of savage dogs. Sable antelopes roam East Africa's grasslands and open woodlands.

**Scimitar oryx**    Males and females have long horns curved like swords called "scimitars." These big antelopes thrive on the parched edges of the Sahara Desert in Africa. Desert oryxes get the moisture they need from juices in the desert plants they eat.
***Threatened Species***

**Pronghorn**    The antelope-like pronghorn is the last of a unique group of North American hoofed mammals. Fifty million pronghorns grazed the prairies until settlers with guns arrived. Only about half a million remain today. One of the fastest long-distance runners, this animal can speed along at 40 miles an hour for about 4 miles without stopping.

**Common duiker**    Any small African antelope seen diving into a thicket is likely to be a duiker of some kind. *Duiker*, in fact, is the South African word for "diver." The duiker eats a variety of foods, including insects, fruits, and grass. It easily disappears into dense undergrowth. The creature is about as heavy as a medium-sized dog but can outrun almost any dog that tries to chase it.

# Odd-toed hoofed mammals, 1

This family includes not only horses but also asses and zebras. All these species once roamed wild across vast open plains. Horses are well designed for this lifestyle. They have sharp front teeth for snipping the tops off grass and long, ridged teeth to crush it into pulp before swallowing. Horses did not evolve special stomachs, as deer and cattle did, but the back end of their gut completes the digestion of tough plant fibers.

A grazing herd of horses will gallop off if disturbed. Each leg is supported only by its middle toe. The other toes shrank and then vanished as the animal evolved. Horses, tapirs, and rhinoceroses form a distinct group of hoofed mammals with an odd number of toes.

**Grévy's zebra**  This is the biggest zebra and the heaviest of all the wild horses. It has more and narrower black stripes than do other zebras. A stiff mane sticks up from its neck and head, and its ears are broad. Northeastern Africa has three separate groups of Grévy's zebra. They mingle with common zebras but do not seem to interbreed with them.
*Threatened Species*

**African wild ass**  This pale creature is a bit larger than a donkey. It is about 4 feet tall. Scientists believe that an extinct North African relative of the wild ass was the donkey's ancestor. Modern wild asses live in small family groups of about 12 animals. They thrive on the edges of scorching deserts in northeastern Africa. They eat the scanty vegetation and travel far to find water. If chased, wild asses show surprising speed. A galloping wild ass can easily outpace a hunter on horseback. Still, hunting has reduced their numbers, as African peoples regard their flesh as a great delicacy.
*Threatened Species*

**Donkey**  The domesticated ass can be gray, brown, almost black, or almost white. Farmers have bred these sure-footed animals for several thousand years to pull or carry loads, mainly in North Africa, southern Europe, and southern Asia. A male donkey (jack) mated with a female horse (mare) produces a mule.

**Common zebra**  Also called the plains zebra or Burchell's zebra, this is the most numerous and widespread species of zebra, found throughout East Africa. A stallion protects up to six mares and their foals. By kicking and biting he may even scare off young lions.

**Przewalski's horse**  In 1879 a Russian explorer named Przewalski saw small wild horses galloping across Mongolia's barren steppes and gave them his name. They are light brown, with stiff black manes. Wild herds have apparently disappeared, but zoos have managed to keep the breed alive.
*Threatened Species*

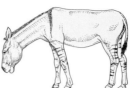

**Asiatic wild ass**  This species, of which there are several varieties, is more horselike than its African relative. Some individuals have black markings on their legs and back. The kiang, a mountain variety, can put on an extra 90 pounds in autumn. This fat provides nourishment when grass is scarce and protects the body against intense winter cold. Asiatic wild asses range across the steppes and deserts of central and southwestern Asia and India. Most herds are nervous and are always on the watch for wolves or human hunters.
*Threatened Species*

**Cape mountain zebra**  The smallest and rarest of the zebras, the mountain zebra has a pattern on its rump resembling the gridiron on a football field. Once abundant in the mountains of southern Africa, by 1937 fewer than 50 were left, all in South Africa's Cape Province. That year a national park was set aside for the zebras, and by the 1980s their number had increased to about 200. Hartmann's zebra, another mountain zebra, is more plentiful.
*Threatened Species*

**Chapman's zebra**  Chapman's zebra is a subspecies of the common zebra. From southeastern Africa, it was named after the first person to send a specimen to England, where it was identified. Its special features include gray stripes between black ones on its hindquarters. It also has fewer markings on its legs than do most common zebras, although its stripes usually go down to its hooves.

# Odd-toed hoofed mammals, 2

With a short neck and a small trunk, the tapir, a pony-sized plant-eater, looks a bit like an elephant. However, its three-toed feet show us that its closest relatives are horses and rhinoceroses.

Tapirs have stocky bodies and short, strong legs that are perfect for pushing through forest undergrowth. Their tiny trunks are useful for sniffing and for pulling leaves down to their mouths. At night they graze in clearings and browse on tender shoots and water plants. All of them enjoy wallowing in pools to cool off and to kill the parasites that live on their skin.

Only four kinds of tapir survive. Three live in South America, the fourth in southeastern Asia.

**Mountain tapir**
Mountain tapirs are the smallest of all the tapirs. They are solidly built and weigh about 500 pounds. They have the short, flexible trunk that is characteristic of tapirs. But only the mountain tapir's snout is covered with dense, bristly hair. Mountain tapirs munch on ferns and other plants in misty mountaintop forests. Peru, Colombia, and Ecuador now have laws forbidding anyone to kill them.
***Threatened Species***

**Baird's tapir**  This plain brown tapir with a narrow mane is also called the giant tapir. The biggest New World tapir, it lives in Central and South America, in habitats ranging from mangrove swamps to mountains more than 10,000 feet high. Like other tapirs, it is becoming scarce as people hunt it for its meat and its tough hide and turn its forest homes into farms.
***Threatened Species***

**Malayan tapir**  This tapir's striking black-and-white pattern helps confuse enemies, which see it only as pale patches in the dim forest light. The young are even more cunningly camouflaged, with pale stripes on a dark body. Malayan tapirs are solitary animals that move quickly through dense bushes, creating trails. They live in the tropical forests of southeastern Asia.

***Threatened Species***

**Brazilian tapir**  Its long, flexible snout helps this tapir tear off twigs, leaves, and shoots in the Amazon rainforest, where it lives. The animal swims well and usually lives near water. If a jaguar leaps on its back, the Brazilian tapir will rush into a clump of bushes, trying to knock the jaguar aside before its teeth and claws can pierce the tapir's tough, bristly hide.

**Evolving tapirs**
The first tapirs were not much bigger or heavier than dogs. One, called *Helalates*, lived in North American and Asian forests 40 million years ago.

Modern tapirs came from ancestors such as *Miotapirus*, which may have had a tiny trunk. This tapir lived in North American forests about 15 million years ago.

Tapirs once lived around the world. Now, great distances separate the three American tapirs from the only kind still found in southeastern Asia.

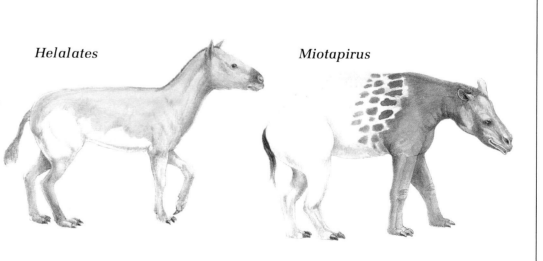

*Helalates*

*Miotapirus*

# Odd-toed hoofed mammals, 3

Rhinoceroses are among the strongest, largest, and most dangerous of all land animals. These massive mammals are built like living tanks. Thick, armorlike skin covers their immense bodies and short, stumpy legs. Their main weapons are the horns on their nose.

Both kinds of African rhinoceros have two long, curved horns right above the nose. All three Asian species have at least one short horn. An angry black rhinoceros may lower its horns and charge hard enough to overturn a small truck. Other kinds of rhinoceros are usually less aggressive. All five are in danger of becoming extinct.

**Black rhinoceros** This big African mammal is actually grayish. It is smaller than the white rhinoceros, although even a black rhinoceros may weigh 2 tons. One of its special features is a flexible upper lip that is used to grasp the leafy twigs it eats. Rhinoceroses are very nearsighted. They smell or hear people before they see them. Quick-tempered, they are quite likely to make a sudden, terrifying charge, puffing like a steam engine as they run.
***Threatened Species***

**Sumatran rhinoceros** This is Asia's only two-horned rhinoceros. Its skin is creased and slightly hairy, a little like the skin of its extinct relative, the woolly rhinoceros of Ice Age Europe. The smallest rhinoceros, it has short, stubby horns and weighs less than a ton. Sumatran rhinoceroses munch on the leaves of young trees and wallow in muddy pools in hilly tropical forests. Zoologists think that only a few hundred individuals are left, all in Sumatra, Borneo, and Malaysia.
***Threatened Species***

**Indian rhinoceros** Nearly as heavy as the white rhinoceros, the Indian rhinoceros has a thick, armorlike hide that lies in folds. Unlike both African species, the Indian rhinoceros has only one horn. Instead of using the horn for fighting, it bites with long, tusklike teeth. Indian rhinoceroses graze and wallow in the swampy grasslands of Nepal and northern India. At mating time the males pant and squeak as they chase the females, which make strange honking noises.
***Threatened Species***

**White rhinoceros** A white rhinoceros is really grayish. To identify it, look for a humped neck and a head ending in a wide, square-lipped mouth just right for cropping grass. It is bigger than the black rhinoceros, weighing as much as 4 tons. Elephants are the only heavier land animals. Despite their huge size and long horns, white rhinoceroses seldom attack people. They would rather curl up their tails and trot away. Only those in southern Africa seem likely to survive.

**Javan rhinoceros** Javan rhinoceroses look like Indian rhinoceroses but are smaller and have a large upper lip for seizing leaves. Once they thrived in lands as far apart as India and Java, but by 1990 hunters had killed off all but a few dozen in western Java's swampy forests. Guards now keep an eye on those left, but zoologists fear that the species cannot survive. The Javan rhinoceros is currently the most endangered of all large mammals.
***Threatened Species***

---

**Rhinoceroses of long ago**
Like tapirs and horses, the first rhinoceroses were small and nimble. North America's *Hyracodon* was about 5 feet long and had slim legs. It lived 25 million years ago.

Some early rhinoceroses evolved into giants such as Asia's *Indricotherium*. *Indricotherium* was the largest land mammal of all time — larger than modern-day elephants. It stood 18 feet tall at the shoulders.

*Hyracodon*

*Indricotherium*

# Rodents, 1

Rodents are generally small, gnawing plant-eaters with front teeth as sharp as chisels. Some species can chew through anything from grass to wood. Squirrels, rats, and mice live on most continents, but there are rodents that live only in the Americas. The following two pages picture 12 New World rodents and 1 Old World relative, the crested porcupine, which comes from Africa.

**Chinchilla**   Soft, dense fur keeps chinchillas warm on cold Andean mountainsides. Trapping them for their fur has made wild chinchillas scarce, but they are bred widely on fur farms.

**Guinea pig**   The stocky, tailless guinea pigs, or cavies, that are kept as pets come from wild South American ancestors. After dark, families of wild cavies leave their burrows and come out to feed. Guinea pigs have few defenses. So when they see an enemy approaching, they quickly scamper underground.

**North American porcupine**
Strong toes and claws help this North American forest rodent creep up trees while eating bark, buds, and twigs. What it lacks in speed it makes up for with its spines, used for defense.

**Crested porcupine**   This African porcupine is as heavy as a medium-sized dog. When threatened, it charges backward and drives its quills deep into an enemy.

**Spiny rat**   Spiny rats are solidly built and have sharp, spiny hairs. They are a little smaller than brown rats and have a much shorter tail. They come from southern Brazil and northern Argentina.

**South American porcupine**   A tail that grips helps this small porcupine climb and hang from branches in the tropical forests of Central and South America. Its spines are short but sharp, and any animal that tries attacking it is quickly turned away.

**Coypu**   Coypus resemble beavers with ratlike tails. These big South American rodents, also called nutrias, dive and swim well with their webbed feet. They burrow in riverbanks and eat water plants. Some that escaped from fur farms in North America and Europe became crop pests.

**Agouti**    About 10 kinds of agoutis live in Central and South America. Less than 18 inches in length, they have long, slim legs and can run very fast. Some can make standing jumps of several yards. Agoutis' tails are so short, they are difficult to see. Most agoutis spend the day eating fallen fruits, roots, or stems. They wear paths in the forest as they walk between their feeding grounds and burrows.

**Paca**    About 2$^1/_2$ feet long, pacas from Central and South America stay during the day in riverbank burrows. At night they come out to munch on roots, stems, and fallen fruits. They often eat crops of cassava and sugarcane. When chased, they may escape by plunging into a stream. People hunt them for their tasty meat, but a cornered paca can give a savage bite.

**Mara**    People also call this the Patagonian hare. With strong hind legs and rabbitlike ears, the long-legged mara does look like a hare. It even runs and bounds like a hare, at up to 20 miles an hour. Its closest relatives, however, are guinea pigs. Maras are similar to hares partly because they live in similar climates. Both are also plant-eaters that prefer wide open spaces, where a quick getaway could save a life. Baby maras are born in the safety of a burrow.

**Capybara**    The world's largest living rodent, which can weigh more than 100 pounds, looks like a cross between a big dog and a guinea pig. Capybaras live in and near South American lakes and rivers. They swim well, using their slightly webbed feet and showing only ears, eyes, and nostrils above the water. Their main foods are water plants.

**Plains vizcacha**    This relative of the chinchilla with a striped face is about as big as a house cat. The male is twice the size of the female and has a long, droopy mustache. On the Argentinian pampas, where plains vizcachas live, up to 50 may share a group of burrows, marked by small rubbish heaps. Farmers have now wiped out many of the colonies. Before this, you could have seen up to 100 colonies anywhere in the pampas.

**Hutia**    About a dozen species of hutia live on Cuba and other Caribbean islands. Hutias are short, rabbit-sized rodents. Some kinds are tasty to eat. They cannot climb very well, and they breed very slowly. Human hunters, dogs, and mongooses have completely killed off some species of hutia, and the surviving ones are at great risk.
***Threatened Species***

# Rodents, 2

Squirrels are furry rodents with large eyes and rounded ears. There are more than 250 species. Only Antarctica and Australia have no squirrels. Tree squirrels, with long, bushy tails, live in woods, where they scamper up tree trunks and leap from tree to tree like little acrobats. Ground squirrels have short tails and live in burrows dug into slopes or into the ground. The largest of the ground squirrels are the marmots, prairie dogs, and woodchucks.

Beavers are larger than marmots. They live in streams in northern North America, swimming with their webbed back feet and steering with their broad, flat tail.

**Marmot**   More than a dozen species of these large, burrowing squirrels live in the northern continents. Alpine marmots bask on sunny mountain slopes and munch on alpine plants. Mountain marmots may spend nearly half the year hibernating deep in hay-lined burrows. The best-known woodland marmot is North America's woodchuck, or groundhog. Like other marmots, it sits up on its haunches to watch for signs of danger. A few other species live on steppes and prairies.

**Indian palm squirrel**   With its three stripes, this squirrel from southern India looks a little like the North American chipmunk. Even in towns it is often seen hanging head down from a tree trunk, making shrill scolding noises. It is a lively creature, scampering up and down branches after palm nuts and other morsels to eat. By sipping nectar, it pollinates the flowers of silky oak trees but it also does damage by munching on cotton tree buds.

**Ground squirrel**   Ground-living squirrels include slimmer, smaller burrowers than the tubby marmots and prairie dogs. Like most of those, ground squirrels live in the grassy plains and mountain meadows of northern Asia and North America. Their favorite foods are seeds, eggs, and insects. What they do not eat at once, they cram into their cheek pouches, to take home and store.

**Indian giant squirrel**   As you walk through a forest in southern India, you might hear a loud call warning you that nearby are some of the world's largest tree squirrels. Including its tail, which is longer than its head and body, an Indian giant squirrel is nearly 3 feet long. Its coat can be off-white, red, or almost black, though some color variations seem to be disappearing. The creature appears to like only certain patches of forest. There it raises its young and sleeps in a large, untidy nest high up in a tree. The Indian giant squirrel is also called the Malabar giant squirrel.

**Red squirrel**   This small, light squirrel has tufted ears and a plume-shaped tail. It scampers and leaps high above the ground, through woods from western Europe to eastern Asia. It sleeps and rears its young in treetop nests built of twigs and leaves. Red squirrels chatter noisily. They remain active all year, eating bark, fruit, fungi, insects, seeds, and birds' eggs.

**Flying squirrel**   Nearly 40 kinds of squirrels, mostly Asian, can stretch the folds of skin between their hands and feet to make their bodies into tiny parachutes. North American species are a little bigger than mice and can glide between trees 30 feet apart. The giant flying squirrel of southeastern Asia can glide the length of four football fields laid end to end.

**African bush squirrel**   Nearly a dozen kinds of bush squirrels live in Africa's grasslands and dry forests. Their coats range from speckled grayish yellow to bright reddish brown in color, and some have stripes. The one shown here is an East African species found at the forest edge.

**Beaver**   Beavers are 3 feet long, are strong swimmers with broad tails and webbed feet, and have teeth like chisels. They will gnaw through trees to cut them down and dig canals to float the logs to a stream. They block the stream with a dam of branches and twigs held together with mud. In the pool that forms, they build a lodge — a mound of twigs and branches. Underwater entrances lead to a chamber where the young are raised. Beavers are most abundant in North America.

# Rodents, 3

One family of rodents, the murids, outnumbers all the rest. Its more than 1,100 species include rats, mice, hamsters, gerbils, and lemmings. Some of these and other small rodents are shown on the following pages. You can find at least a few of them living almost anywhere, from fields and forests to deserts and swamps — even in buildings.

All murids can burrow, climb, leap, run, and swim. They can also eat huge quantities of seeds, leaves, stems, and roots. Because they steal stored and growing grain, rats and mice are considered huge farm pests. However, farmers cannot kill them all, because they are small enough to hide easily and they breed extremely fast.

**House mouse** Often house mice live inside hollow walls in buildings. However, they probably came from a wild subspecies that still lives on the grasslands of Central Asia. These mice may have begun stealing food from farming settlements more than 6,000 years ago. House mice later stowed away on trading ships and spread around the world.

**Yellow-necked mouse** This creature looks like a large, richly colored wood mouse with a big yellow spot on its chest. An agile climber, it has sometimes been seen high in tall forest trees. It appears in European gardens and orchards and often finds its way indoors.

**Harvest mouse** One of the smallest rodents, this European and Asian mouse is so light that it can climb up certain grasses. Gripping the stems with its tail, it weaves a grass nest the size of a tennis ball. Inside, the female gives birth to up to nine young as tiny as bees. The American harvest mouse is the same size but is not a close relative.

**Wood mouse** This European and Asian mouse with large ears and big, bright eyes looks like the yellow-necked mouse but climbs less. Sometimes it bounds along, all of its feet off the ground at once.

**Rock mouse** The dry, rocky hills and woods of northern Greece and nearby countries are where you find this relative of the wood mouse. It is big enough to be mistaken for a young rat, but rats have smaller hind feet for their size.

**Striped field mouse** A distinctive long black stripe running down its back and a tail a little shorter than its head and body show this cannot be a wood mouse. It lives from Central Europe east to China.

**Cretan spiny mouse** Some predators that try to eat spiny mice spit them out because of the stiff, sharp hairs. The skin itself is soft, and the tail snaps off easily. Outside of the Greek island of Crete, most spiny mice live in Africa and Asia.

**Desert jerboa** No bigger than a large mouse, this rodent looks like a miniature kangaroo bounding across the Sahara Desert on huge hind legs. It balances and steers with its long, tufted tail. At top speed, jerboas can leap 9 feet and outrun a cantering horse.

**Black rat** Long ago these southeastern Asian rats spread around the world on ships and invaded the buildings in ports. With the black rats came the fleas that infected millions of people with bubonic plague and other deadly diseases. Today these rats are less common than they were and may even have died out in places.

**Brown or Norway rat** Brown rats are from Asia but have spread almost everywhere. They are hated pests, stealing and spoiling stored food and also spreading diseases. Brown rats breed faster than black rats. Instead of climbing onto roofs, brown rats prefer to live in sewers and cellars.

**African pygmy mouse** This seems to be one of the world's smallest rodents, but some scientists suspect it is only one of several tiny species. Another kind of pygmy mouse lives in East Africa on grasslands often swept by fire. Most of the mice survive the flames by hiding in their burrows.

**Three-toed jerboa** Several species of these little kangaroo-like rodents live on the dry plains of Central Asia. Some spend the day hiding safely in burrows, only coming out at night to hop around and feed. A three-toed species from the Gobi Desert has a head and body even shorter than the jerboa's.

**Meadow jumping mouse**  There are more than a dozen kinds of jumping mice. This North American species has a tail almost twice as long as its body and moves along in short bursts, searching for seeds and insects.

**Golden hamster**  This is a fat, short-tailed rodent. Wild golden hamsters live in parts of Europe and Asia. At night they stuff their immense cheek pouches with plant food to take to their underground nests.

**Dormouse**  As it climbs up through a hedge, this European rodent looks a bit like a squirrel, but it is smaller than a house mouse. In autumn, dormice stuff themselves with nuts and berries until they grow quite plump. Their body fat must nourish them all winter while they hibernate, curled up inside a grassy nest. Hibernating dormice breathe so slowly, they seem to be dead.

**Gerbil**  More than 90 kinds of gerbils live in African and Asian grasslands and deserts. To save water, they produce very little urine, so they are cleaner pets than most rodents.

**Desert kangaroo rat**  These North American rodents bounce about like tiny kangaroos. They never drink, getting the moisture they need from the plants they eat. They live in the deserts of northwestern Mexico and the southwestern United States.

**Muskrat**  North America's muskrats look like big rats, but they spend much of their time in water, paddling with their hind feet and flattened tail. Some live on lakes in piles of plants.

**Norway lemming**  The thick snow above its burrow traps heat, helping keep this active little Arctic rodent warm in winter as it digs for roots, stems, leaves, and berries. Every three or four years, Norway lemmings breed so fast that many must set off to find new homes. The migrating lemmings cross streams and rivers. Thousands drown swimming out to sea.

**Mitchell's hopping mouse** This is Australia's answer to the North American kangaroo rat. The mouse walks on all fours, but if startled, it hops away at high speed. It can jump sideways, too. The creature lives in a nest down a long, steep burrow. The burrow has an even steeper escape route that runs almost straight up.

**Giant Gambian pouched rat** One of the world's largest rats, this one grows nearly 3 feet long, including its tail, and is as heavy as a small dog. It lives in wooded plains across much of Africa. Each rat lives in a burrow with several entrances. Africans often dig out the big, meaty rodents to eat.

**Plains pocket gopher** This North American burrower uses its cheek pouches as pockets, stuffing them with shoots or roots to eat in its burrow. Sometimes whole plants vanish underground, tugged down from below to be chewed up by the rodent's sharp front teeth.

**Spring hare** This unusual animal looks like a cross between a hare, a squirrel, and a kangaroo. As big as a small dog, it burrows with its front paws, feeds on all fours, and bounds along on its hind legs. Spring hares can be found throughout Africa. Because they come out only at night, few people see them.

**Crested rat** Crested rats are climbing rodents that live in the mountain forests of northeastern Africa. Their name comes from a strip of coarse hair running down their back. A scared crested rat raises this mane and exposes a scent gland that gives off a strong, unpleasant odor.

**Dassie rat**
The dassie rats of southwestern Africa look a little like small squirrels, and they behave like hyraxes. Dassies live in colonies that bask on rocks and move about to keep in the sun. One dassie rat from the colony keeps watch and warns the others with a shrill cry if it sees an eagle or a mongoose.

**Naked mole rat** This mole rat is the only rodent with almost no hair. In sandy parts of East Africa, colonies of up to 100 of these ugly, wrinkled creatures live together underground like ants. Workers dig for roots while "courtiers" tend a queen — the only female that produces young.

# Rabbits, hares, and pikas

People once thought these mammals were rodents. Like rodents, they have front teeth shaped like chisels, which keep growing as they wear down. But rabbits have two pairs of upper front teeth (rodents have only one), a stumpy tail, and long, narrow ears. Hares, which include jackrabbits, have even longer ears and very long, strong hind legs. Because pikas are smaller than hares, with short, round ears like a mouse's, they are sometimes known as mouse hares.

Most pikas live on mountains. Rabbits and hares live in grassy places. Some rabbits spend all day in burrows, coming out to feed at dawn or dusk. Rabbits hide from danger in their burrows; hares make high-speed escapes. The burrows are refuges for baby rabbits, born blind, naked, and helpless. Hares are born more self-sufficient, with their eyes open and with fur.

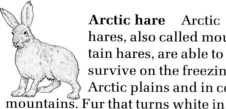

**Brown hare**   The saying "mad as a March hare" comes from the antics that brown hares perform. When several meet, females drive off males that bother them by bucking, leaping, kicking, and even rearing on their hind legs and throwing punches. Brown hares usually live alone. By day they crouch in the long grass. A dog can almost be standing on the hare before it races away, dodging to and fro to put off its pursuer. Brown hares live in Europe, Asia, and Africa. You can tell them apart from Old World rabbits by their extra-long ears and hind legs.

**Arctic hare**   Arctic hares, also called mountain hares, are able to survive on the freezing Arctic plains and in cold mountains. Fur that turns white in winter makes these animals hard to see in the snow. This helps them hide from hungry foxes and owls. Toes that spread wide apart help them escape quickly over soft snow. Body heat would be lost from the surface of ears as long as a brown hare's; the ears of these hares are shorter.

**Snowshoe rabbit**   Stiff bristles on the hind feet serve as snowshoes to stop these hares (not rabbits, in spite of their name) from sinking into the snow. Also called varying hares, they go from brown in summer to white in winter. Snowshoe rabbits live in the northern forests of North America, where they nibble leaves, shoots, and bark. If a lynx attacks a resting hare, the hare immediately speeds off at more than 25 miles an hour. Every 10 years or so these hares grow very plentiful, and within only a short time, so do the lynxes that eat them. Then most of the hares die off, leaving many lynxes to starve.

**Black-tailed jackrabbit** Enormously long ears that work like radiators help to control this creature's body temperature. In very hot weather, blood fills the vessels in its ears. From the blood, heat flows into the ears and out into the air. In this way the animal keeps comfortably cool. Black-tailed jackrabbits live in North America's southwestern deserts and dry grasslands.

**Northern pika**   Rocky mountain slopes in North America and Asia are home to this relative of the hares and rabbits. Northern pikas are no bigger than rats, with legs much shorter than those of rabbits. They cannot run fast, so they keep a sharp lookout for enemies. If one sees an eagle coming, it warns its neighbors with a high, piping cry. Northern pikas live in colonies among the rocks. In autumn they pile grass into heaps to dry and store it in burrows. This hay becomes their winter food supply.

**European rabbit** European rabbits are fast breeders, forming colonies that contain many burrows. If grass or other food is plentiful, their numbers multiply quickly. Two rabbits can produce 70,000 young in two years. Rabbits can become pests by eating the grass that farmers need for livestock. When they were let loose by European settlers in Australia, the rabbits turned huge pastures into deserts. Cottontails of North and South America are similar to the European rabbit. They do not live in burrows, however.

**Red pika**   Three kinds of pikas have their coat colors in their names. The Turkestan red pika lives in high mountains north of Pakistan. The Chinese red pika lives in eastern Tibet and nearby. The Afghan pika from Afghanistan has the scientific name *rufescens*, which means "reddish."

**Steppe pika**   Unlike most pikas, this kind does not flourish on rocky mountain slopes. It lives on the grassy steppes of Russia and Kazakhstan. Like other pikas, steppe pikas utter thin, bleating cries and carry hay underground as winter food. None of the pikas seems to hibernate.

# Index

## A

aardvark 62–63
aardwolf 32
Afghan pika *see* red pika
African buffalo 72
African bush squirrel 86–87
African civet 40–41
African elephant 62–63
African hunting dog 34–35
African pygmy mouse 88–89
African wild ass 78–79
African yellow-winged bat 18–19
agile gibbon *see* white-handed gibbon
agouti 85
Allen's swamp monkey 27
alpaca 67
Alpine marmot *see* marmot
Amazon river dolphin 58
American badger 42–43
American black bear 36–37
angwantibo 21
anteaters 10–13, 59
antelopes 73, 74–77
apes 20, 30–31
Arabian oryx 76
Arctic fox 35
Arctic hare 92–93
armadillos 59–61
artiodactyls 64–77
Asiatic black bear 36–37
Asiatic wild ass 78–79
asses 78–79
Atlantic humpbacked dolphin 57
Atlantic seal *see* gray seal
aye-aye 22–23

## B

babirusa 64
baboons 27, 29
Bactrian camel 67
badgers 42–43
baiji 58
Baikal seal 53
Baird's tapir 80–81
bald ouakari 24–25
baleen whales 54–55
banded anteater *see* numbat
banded mongoose 33
Barbary ape 27
Barbary sheep 73
Baringo giraffe 70–71
bat-eared fox 34–35
bats 17–19
bearded seal 52
bears 32, 36–37
beaver 86–87
beluga 56
Benguela dolphin 57
big cats 48–51
black bear 36–37
black dolphin 57
black lemur 22–23
black porpoise 57
black rat 88–89
black rhinoceros 82–83
black spider monkey 24
black-and-white colobus monkey 28
black-backed jackal 34
black-capped capuchin 24–25
black-chin dolphin 57
black-footed cat 46–47
black-footed ferret 44
black-tailed jackrabbit 92–93
blue duiker 74
blue whale 55
blue wildebeest *see* brindled gnu

bobcat 45
bontebok 76–77
bottlenose dolphin 57
bouto *see* Amazon river dolphin
bowhead whale 54
brahman *see* zebu
Brazilian tapir 80–81
brindled gnu 76–77
brown bear 36–37
brown capuchin *see* black-capped capuchin
brown hare 92–93
brown hyena 32
brown long-eared bat 18
brown rat 88–89
brush-tailed phascogale 12–13
brush-tailed possum 10–11
Bryde's whale 54
buffalo 72
bulldog bat *see* Mexican fishing bat
Burchell's zebra *see* common zebra
Burmeister's armadillo *see* greater fairy armadillo
Burmeister's porpoise *see* black porpoise
bush babies 20–21

## C

Californian sea lion 52
camels 67
Cape golden mole 16
Cape mountain zebra 78–79
capuchin monkeys 24
capybara 85
caracal 46–47
caribou *see* reindeer
carnivores 32–53
Caspian tiger 50–51
*catarrhines* 27–29
cats 32, 45–47
cattle 72
cavy *see* guinea pig
chamois 73
Chapman's zebra 78–79
cheetah 48–49
chevrotains 68
Chilean dolphin *see* black dolphin
chimpanzee 30–31
chinchilla 84
Chinese ferret-badger 42–43
Chinese muntjac deer 68–69
Chinese red pika *see* red pika
Chinese river dolphin *see* baiji
Chinese water deer 68–69
civets 32, 40–41
clouded leopard 48–49
coati 38–39
collared peccary 64–65
colubus monkeys 28
colugos 17
Commerson's dolphin 56
common duiker 76–77
common gibbon *see* white-handed gibbon
common marmoset 26
common mole 14–15
common opossum 10
common rorqual *see* finback whale
common squirrel monkey 24–25
common wambenger *see* brush-tailed phascogale
common zebra 78–79
Coquerel's mouse lemur 22–23
cottontail rabbit *see* European rabbit
cougar *see* puma
coyotes 34–35
coypu 84
crabeater seal 53
crested porcupine 84
crested rat 91

Cretan spiny mouse 88–89
cusimanse 33

## D

Dall sheep 73
dassie rat 91
deer 68–69
desert jerboa 88–89
desert kangaroo rat 90
Diana monkey 29
dingo 34–35
dogs 32, 34–35
dolphins 55–58
donkey 78–79
dormouse 90
dromedary 67
dugong 62
duiker 74 *and see* common duiker

## E

eared seals 32, 52–53
earless seals 32, 52–53
echidna *see* spiny anteater
edentates 59–60
elephant seal 52
elephants 62–63
elk 68–69
emperor tamarin 26
Eurasian badger 42–43
Eurasian otter 42–43
European elk *see* moose
European rabbit 92–93
even-toed hoofed mammals 64–77

## F

false killer whale 56
fennec fox 34–35
ferret-badgers 42–43
finback whale 55
finless porpoise 58
fishing cat 45
flatheaded cat 45
flying fox 17
flying lemurs *see* colugos
flying squirrel 86–87
forest elephant shrew 14–15
fossa 40
foul-marten *see* polecat
foxes 34–35
franciscana 58
fruit bats 17–19
fur seals 52–53

## G

galagos 20–21
Galápagos sea lion 52
gaur 72
gelada 29
gemsbok 76–77
genets 40–41
*Genetta victoriae see* giant genet
gerbil 88, 90
gerenuk 76–77
giant anteater 59
giant armadillo 60–61
giant eland 74
giant flying squirrel *see* flying squirrel
giant forest hog 64–65
giant Gambian pouched rat 91
giant genet 40–41
giant otter shrew 16

94

DEP.-LEG. Nº B-29.418-92